Bound

Kitten & Sunshine Anderson

PUBLISHED BY FANTAISIOCHT PUBLISHING, MISSISSIPPI

Ebook ASIN: B0CCXN1WGP

Paperback **ISBN:** 979-8853830486

Hard Cover **ISBN:** 9798882766138

First print in paperback in July 2023 and hardcover February 2024

Cover Design by Fantaisioct Publishing

Edited by Gloria Titler

Published by Fantaisioct Publishing, Biloxi, Mississippi

Printed in the United States of America

Contents

Warning

This book is not based on real events or people.

This book contains intense fantasy scenes of hard kinks/edgeplay, graphic sex, and harsh language. It is intended only for an adult audience. Beware: this is a dark, weird, kinky read. The activities depicted therein are dangerous and are not meant to be an example of realistic BDSM. Reader discretion is advised.

Kinks/Fetishes within: erotic humiliation, fearplay, painplay, knifeplay, consensual non-consent (CNC), orgasm denial, boot worship, spanking, crying, blowjobs, group sexual activities, bondage, public play, fire play.

This book also contains graphic traumatic rape scenes.

Prologue

ZayShawn-

My mind wanders as I sit here, claiming the final blows that will set me free.

What will she be like? I can't wait to claim her as mine! I can almost see her in my mind, her creamy white silky skin bound in my leather cuffs attached to the dark oak St. Andrew's cross waiting for my pleasure...

The next blow from the whip pulled ZayShawn from his thoughts.

"Pay attention, Pet! Your thoughts should only be on me. How are you going to care for your own submissive if you can't even control your mind from wandering? Things like this will get your submissive injured," said the mysterious feminine voice.

Knowing his vital mistake, ZayShawn bowed his head respectfully. "Sorry, Mistress, it will not happen again."

The next thing ZayShawn heard was the bullwhip snapping next to his head.

"Five more lashes, Pet, and I will release you from your bonds. Now count."

ZayShawn counted each bite from the Mistress's whip that crossed his milk chocolate skin.

"One, Mistress."

"Two, Mistress."

"Three, Mistress."

"Good Boy, now the next two lashes will be testing. Are you willing to wear my mark for the last time, Pet?" asked the Domme.

"Yes, Mistress, it would be an honor," he replied in a low baritone voice.

When the next strike hit, ZayShawn grunted, "Four, Mistress."

After the final strike, ZayShawn was just on the edge of subspace.

"Five, Mistress."

Once ZayShawn was uncuffed, he bowed at his Domme's feet and said, "Thank you, Mistress."

The Domme looked down at her sub and said, "Rise, Pet, and kiss your master."

Without a word, ZayShawn stood, and when he went to kiss his Domme, she turned her head and offered her cheek. She stepped back and smiled, "Go, my Pet, I release you. You are now free to find your own submissive. But remember, her welfare comes first. Do not dishonor our community by forgetting your training."

"Yes, Mistress Raven. I will remember my training."

"ZayShawn, you are no longer my submissive. You may call me Brenna," she said, smiling.

As ZayShawn left, he noticed Brenna was working with a new sub. This one was a female, and he could tell she was very new to the lifestyle. He hit the button and made his McLaren come alive. He smiled as the engine quieted to a purr. He rolled the windows down, turned up the music, and headed to FETISH.

As Abbey sits on her four-post bed leaning against her pillows, staring out of the window, thinking about how, now that she has graduated from college, she is ready to leave the small town where she has lived for her entire life, the sound of her phone ringing brought her out of her thoughts.

Abbey looked down at her cell phone and saw the name of her childhood best friend appear on the screen. However, James Brewer was more like a brother to Abbey than just her best friend. Abbey grew up an only child, and James, a few years older than her, took her under his wing as her protector from the moment they met. James would countless times fight anyone who tried to bully her.

"James Brewer?! Is that really you?" she answered the video call cheerfully.

"Hey, bitch! What are you doing?"

"Just sitting here in boring ass Middlesboro. What's been going on with you? I want to know everything!"

"Well, bitch, I prefer to go by Chuckalisa by night. I am a business-owning Domme drag queen."

"Wait, what?"

"Yes. I am the proud owner of Chuckalisa's Chicken Tits and Waffles in Dallas. I finally found my inner happiness and now know who I am, a badass drag queen who likes to whip bad little boys and the occasional bad little girl."

"What the Fuck?! You waited until now to tell me?"

"Honestly, I was afraid to let anyone know about my sexuality. You know where we come from; being bi-sexual is not exactly accepted. Besides, I didn't know what you would think, and I couldn't bear the thought of you not accepting me."

"James, nothing in this world you could say to me would make me not love and accept you. You are my big-headed big brother. I love you, Muthafuk!"

James smiled, knowing that his "baby sister" was being genuine. "I love you, too, you beautiful Muthafuk!"

"I have missed that smile! So, tell me more about Ms. Chuckalisa."

"I have a much better idea. You grab your bitch crew and bring your asses to Dallas."

Part I

Dominance

"A gentleman holds my hand. A man pulls my hair. A soulmate will do both." —— **Alessandra Torre**

Chapter 1

Abbey excitedly begins a group video call with her best friends, Ava, Hannah, and Sara. As each young woman answered, the butterflies in Abbey's stomach fluttered faster.

"Hey, Abbey!" Ava shrieked.

After each girl answered, they cried simultaneously, "We did it!!!"

"Yes, we did. Now, I have a proposition for you guys," Abbey said nervously.

"Uh-Oh," said Hannah.

Sara sat looking at the screen, waiting for Abbey to speak.

"You all know I have always wanted to leave this small assed podunk town. Well, an opportunity has fallen in my lap."

"What is it, bitch?" asked Ava.

"Well, you all remember James Brewer, right?"

"Yea, he left five years ago, right?" asked Sara.

"Yes. Well, he called me last night and invited us all to come to Dallas. Now, I know how you all are, and I have already looked into jobs for us all, and they are hiring like mad in Dallas for exactly what we each graduated for," she babbled.

Ava was the first to respond. She was always Abbey's ride-or-die friend. "Bitch, I'm down! Anything to get me the hell out of here!"

"I'm down. I can take the bar exam anywhere," exclaimed Hannah.

Of course, Sara hesitated. "I don't know. We won't have any family there. And the only person we would know besides each other is James, and I wasn't ever as close to him as you are. And where will we stay?"

"Bitch, live a little!" commented Hannah.

"Plus, WE are your family!" snarled Ava.

Abbey said, "Sara, I have already looked, and they have a job opening for an aquatic vet at the aquarium. That is EXACTLY what you want to do. And you know you won't get anything like that living here. Besides, you know I have already figured out housing for us!"

"But we know nothing about Dallas," whined Sara.

"Well, you have until tomorrow to think about it because the truck will be packed and pulling out of here at midnight tomorrow night. After that, you can stay here alone if you want to!" stated Abbey.

"Bitch, I am already packed! I'll be there TONIGHT! Shotgun, bitches!!" cheered Ava.

"I have to say bye to Mom, so I will be there in the morning," replied Hannah.

"I don't know. Ya'll would really leave me? I'm just not sure about the risk," said Sara.

"Dueces, Bitch!! We'll send you a postcard," screamed Ava and Abbey in unison.

The girls all hung up, and Abbey packed what little she had left and contacted a car rental company for an SUV for the drive and U-Haul to get a trailer to haul everyone's stuff to Dallas.

Abbey had just finished eating her lunch when her phone rang." Hey, Bitch!"

"Bitch, you gonna have to pick my ass up! I don't have room for all my shit!" yelled Ava.

"Yea, I have to go pick up the truck, and we gotta go get the trailer from U-Haul, too," replied Abbey.

"Okay, so... what are you waiting on?" said Ava.

"I'll be right over."

Abbey and Ava arrived at the house around 8 pm and began loading their things. They sat up for most of the night, talking about all the excitement that was in store for them in Dallas. The next morning they woke up to Hannah screaming, "Wake Up BITCHES!!"

The girls rolled over and said at the same time, "Bitch, shut the fuck up!"

"What fucking time is it, anyway?" asked Abbey.

Hannah said, "It is 9 am. I have already said my goodbyes and packed all of my shit! I am ready to go!"

"Hoe, we have to wait to see if Sara's ass is gonna go, so chill. Besides, we ain't leaving till midnight," said Abbey.

"Go make us some food, Wench!" said Ava, "And don't forget the fucking go-go juice!!"

The trio prepared for their drive to Dallas. As they were finishing up the last of the packing in the U-Haul, they saw a big Ford F-250 pull into Abbey's driveway. Confused, they stood and watched, waiting for the passenger to leave the truck. Finally, Sara asked, "Is there room for my shit?"

Hannah replies, "Yea, your stuff can go in the back seat, and your ass can go in the trailer."

Sara laughed and said, "Bitch, you can go in the trailer!"

The girls all laughed as Sara's dad loaded her stuff into the U-Haul, and at precisely midnight, the four friends started their journey to a new beginning.

ZayShawn could still feel the sting from Mistress Raven's bullwhip as he sat in the club owned by his father and his submissive, sipping on his Crown Apple and Sprite. ZayShawn felt a sense of pride because he had just graduated from Mistress Raven's Red Room Academy, an elite academy where only the most promising Doms attend.

His father walked up to him with his submissive on his arm and congratulated him, "Son, I am so proud of you! I knew you could do it!"

"Thank you, Dad."

"Now, you just have to find your submissive."

"Dad, I am not in any rush. I will know the one when I find her. But she has to be the right one. I want a submissive for life, not just for a short time. I want a love like you have found with Faye." responded ZayShawn.

"I completely understand, son. Just enjoy yourself in the meantime."

"I will, Dad."

Mr. Williams led his submissive through the crowd, leaving ZayShawn to his thoughts.

"I wonder when she will come. Will I be a good Dom? Will she love me? I have so many questions and no answers."

His brothers and best friend, Xavier, Terrance, and Brad, interrupted Zayshawn's thoughts.

"What's up, bro?" asked Xavier.

"Just chillin," replied ZayShawn.

"We're proud of you, youngin," said Terrance.

"Thanks, man."

"You scoping out the prospects?" asked Brad.

"Nah. I want to chill and celebrate, man. I'm not thinking about none of these sack chasers."

The group of friends laughed. Zayshawn was the youngest of three boys. At 28 years old, he was also the youngest graduate of the academy. All his brothers and Brad had already graduated and had multiple submissives, as they weren't trying to settle down with just one. Not ZayShawn; he wanted to settle down and have long-term love and family and would not settle for anything less.

Chapter 2

Not long after, they were on the road. Abbey, Ava, and Hannah jammed to music while Sara sawed logs in the back seat.

"So, where are we headed in Dallas?" asked Hannah.

"All I know is we are heading to Maple Wood Estates. When we get there, I will call him," said Abbey as she channel-surfed.

"If you don't quit with the channel-surfing, I am going to fucking scream. You do this all the time. Just turn on your apple music. We all know you do that, anyway," bitched Ava.

"Shut the fuck up, Wench, and pick a playlist then," Abbey said, tossing her phone to Ava.

"Oooh, play that song," Hannah said, leaning between the seats.

"What song?" asked Ava.

"Bitch, you know what song she wants. She always wants us to play, *'You're a Fucking Bitch.'* So play it and shut up, or you're going in the trailer," Abbey laughed.

Hannah smiled as she looked at a sleeping Sara, reached between the seats, and turned the radio to blasting. Sara covered her head with a travel pillow and gave Hannah the middle finger, making them laugh.

A couple of hours later, the only ones awake were Abbey and Ava.

"Now that the other two are asleep, I can ask some questions," Ava said, grinning and rubbing her hands together.

"I am an open book to you. What do you want to know?" answered Abbey.

"So, if I remember correctly, wasn't James the guy you always hung out with, then disappeared when he graduated?" asked Ava

"That would be correct," she smiled.

"Where did he go? He just fell off the face of the earth. I don't remember him that well. I remember he was like a pit bull when it came to you. You fell into a slump after he graduated because he disappeared."

"So, what is your question?"

"Abbs, I know he means a lot to you. I would never try to come between you two. But you are the other part of me. I would lose my shit if anything ever happened to you. I love the bitches in the back seat, but you are my main bitch. So I guess my question is...What are you going to do if he disappears again?"

"It warms my heart that you are worried about me. But I can tell you that will not happen this time."

"How can you be so sure?"

"Well, he is different now. He found his inner happiness; to do that, he had to leave our small town."

"Okay, I am all ears now. Tell me everything," she said, turning in the seat.

"Remember how quiet he was, how he would only talk to me and you guys sometimes? James differs from the rest of us; he felt like he could never fit in."

"Why? From what I remember, he was a nice guy."

"Yes, James has an enormous heart. He would help anyone; he would even help his worst enemy. But did you ever notice that he never had a girlfriend?"

"Yea. Others always thought you two were together, but I could tell he didn't play on the right side of the field. When we were in high school, I knew he was gay."

"That's why he left," Abbey said sadly.

"Because he is gay? That is ridiculous...we would have accepted him for who he is."

"You know the town we are from would have never accepted him. So he went to Dallas and is living his best life. James told me he is now a business-owning Drag Queen, Domme."

"He's a what? What kind of business? Being a Drag Queen, I get it, but what the hell is a Domme?" asked Ava.

"I know the place is called Chuckalisa's Chicken Tits and Waffles. We will figure out what a Domme is when we get there."

"So I know you said you figured everything out before you called us, and you know I am down for anything. But where are we staying when we get there?"

"We will stay with James. He invited all of us to come and join him in Dallas."

"Sounds good to me. So, what time should we wake these bitches up to get some food?"

"We are two hours from Memphis. So we can stop there."

"Sounds good to me."

Just as the sun rose, Abbey remembered the day James had left.

~June 20th 2018~

Abbey watched James' Ford Ranger disappear around the corner and head to the highway. He promised he would call and come back to visit, but she knew he would never return to the small town of Middlesboro. So not only was she losing her best friend, but she was also losing her protector and

brother. Even though she wished him well and hoped he found happiness,
she desperately wanted to be selfish and ask him to stay. She knew James
was gay, but no one else did. James hid it well. Abbey even hid it from
James that she knew the truth. Nothing in this world could ever make
her not love or accept James. For months after James left, Abbey felt like
a piece of her was missing.

"I've got to pee," Hannah said, pulling Abbey from her thoughts.

"Cross your legs. We are stopping for food in just a couple of miles," said Ava.

"Where are we?" Sara asked.

"Well, good morning, sleepyhead. We are pulling into Memphis," Abbey said, smiling.

Abbey pulled off the exit and said," I hope you guys are ready for some Waffafelley House!"

The girls all said in unison, "Of course, DUH!!"

The girls got out of the SUV, and while Hannah went to the bathroom, the other girls were seated. They looked over the menu as if they had never eaten there before, even though they all knew what they would order from the moment they walked in. Finally, Hannah joined them and said, "Why are you bitches even looking? Ya'll know the menu like the back of your hands."

The other girls laughed, and Ava said, "You're right."

The server approached the foursome and asked with her deep southern drawl, "What'll you ladies have?"

Abbey was the first to speak up, "I will have a sausage egg and cheese grit bowl with a side of bacon and a coffee, please. Lots of cream and sugar."

Ava was next. "I will have a waffle with peanut butter and chocolate chips and a side of bacon. And just a little coffee with my cream and sugar."

Sara chimed in, "Bitch, how do you eat all of that and still stay so thin? I will have the All-Star breakfast with scrambled cheesy eggs, bacon, and my hash browns covered, chunked, and country, please. And I will take a sweet tea."

Hannah then took her turn and said, "I want an All-Star with scrambled eggs, sausage, and all-the-way hash browns. And I will take a coffee as well, please."

"Well, since we are waiting, I wanted to thank you, Abbey, for giving us all this opportunity. I know I was initially acting a bit stank about it, but now that I have thought about it, I am excited to see what the future holds. I love you, Bitch!!"

"Awww, you're welcome, sappy ass! I love you, too!" replied Abbey.

The girls ate their food and discussed what they hoped would happen once they arrived in Dallas. Once they finished eating, Abbey let Ava drive for a while so she could rest. "Bitch, don't wreck my truck or kill us all!!"

"Bitch, why are you letting this bitch drive?" yelled Hannah

"Bitch, because you sure the fuck ain't driving my damn truck! You think cars swim, bitch!!" laughed Abbey.

They paid the check, gassed up the truck, and headed toward Dallas.

Chapter 3

As Ava pulled off the exit in Dallas, she woke Abbey up. "Wake up, sleepyhead. We're in Dallas, and we all have to pee."

Abbey stretched her arms above her head. "We're here already? Bitch, did you put Red Bull in the damn tank?"

"No. You were exhausted, so I didn't wake you when we stopped."

"Thanks, Sis. Now I have to pee and call James."

The girls piled out of the SUV and headed to the bathroom.

"It's hot as hell here!" stated Sara

"Yea, a total difference from Kentucky," said Hannah.

Once they all got cold drinks and returned to the car, Abbey called James. When she saw her brother's face, she could only smile.

"Hey, you!!" exclaimed James. "Where are you?"

"We're in Dallas. What's the address?"

James quickly gave her the address and said, "I'll see you soon! I'll text you the code."

Abbey quickly said okay and hung up before putting James' address into the GPS. Abbey pulled out of the gas station with butterflies at the thought of seeing her long-time best friend and brother.

As the girls pulled into Maple Wood Estates, they were all in awe of the beautiful homes before them. Abbey followed the GPS directions, smiling, and thought, *"Wow, he must be doing good for himself if he lives here. He is gonna have to do a lot of explaining!"*

They pulled to the address, and a huge gate blocked their way. Abbey approached a speaker box with a keypad just outside the gate. She looked into her phone to find the text that James had sent to her. Tears filled her eyes when she realized the numbers. She punched in the number 0619, her birthday.

Ava looked at Abbey as they rounded the circular drive and said, " What kind of business did you say he owns? Bitch, I scared!"

"He owns Chuckalisa's Chicken Tits and Waffles; that's all I know," said a confused Abbey.

"Bitch, for all you know, he is a drug runner, and that waffle place is just a front, and we all gonna die!" cried Hannah.

"Or end up in prison!" added Sara.

"At least we'll all be together!" said Ava.

As they pulled up to the door, Abbey spotted James. He looked just as she remembered him, except he had a bald head and a leaner, muscular build. Abbey couldn't contain her excitement and barely got the truck in park before she jumped out and ran full speed into James' arms. James picked her up and spun her around. "God, I missed you, baby girl!"

They embraced for what seemed like forever when James finally said, "Now let me look at you."

Abbey let go of his neck and stepped back. James took her hand, spun her around, and gave her his nod of approval before leaning down and whispering to her, "How much have you told them?"

"Only Ava knows all that I know."

He nodded, looked at the other girls, and said, "Come inside; I have something to tell you after the tour."

When the girls entered the door, their eyes grew as large as saucers. James had a beautiful six-bedroom and five-bathroom home. There were chandeliers in every room and king-sized beds with the best linens. The floors were heated marble throughout the whole house. There was an Olympic-sized swimming pool with a 10-person hot tub. The girls noticed their names on the different room doors, with Abbey's on the one closest to James' room.

Once they finished the tour, James led the girls into the family room and told them to sit down. "So, I know that all of you nosey asses want some answers, and now you will get them. I left Middlesboro in 2018 because I knew I could never truly be who I am there. I am a bi-sexual drag queen Domme. I own a VERY lucrative restaurant slash strip club named Chuckalisa's Chicken Tits and Waffles. I am James by day and Chuckalisa by night. And if you guys aren't comfortable with that, then there is no need for you to unpack."

Ava stood up, walked over, and threw her arms around him. "Baby, I knew all of that about you when we were in school. I didn't feel the need to voice it to you until you were ready."

Sara and Hannah stood up, walked over to him, and said, "We accept you for who you are, James, and would love to get to know the real you!"

As they all sat back down, Abbey stood with her arms crossed and said, "Well, I don't like it! I love it! And I love you, James!" as she smiled.

James smiled, grabbed her by the waist, playfully picked her up, and tossed her onto the plush couch. They all laughed as James jumped on Abbey and acted like he was fighting her.

"I don't know about ya'll, but I need a shower," said Abbey.

"You will all find toiletries and towels in your respective bathrooms," said James. "Please tell me you hoe's properly labeled all those boxes so my, um... 'guys' can unload that gaudy U-Haul."

"Yes," they said in unison.

The girls went to the truck to grab their overnight bags containing a change of clothes and took off up the stairs to their respective rooms.

All the rooms were laid out the same. Each one had a complete sitting room with a flat-screen tv and fireplace. Off of the sitting room were the bedroom and en suite. Inside the bedroom were the most beautiful king-sized beds. The bathroom is complete with an extra deep oval tub in front of a window overlooking the expansive yard, the shower big enough for two encased in glass. As each girl entered their room, you could hear them shrieking in delight.

As Abbey walked into her room, she was in total shock. She could tell that James had this room prepared especially for her. The entire room was decked out in pink silks with a Paris theme. When she walked into the bedroom, she looked at the bed and spotted a large character pillow of her favorite character, Grogu. Then, as she ventured into the bathroom, she spotted the biggest bottle of her favorite perfume she had ever seen sitting on the counter, along with an entire set of bath products. Abbey squealed in delight as she picked up the bottle to smell the sweet scent of Versace Bright Crystal.

Abbey ran a hot bath and added some bubble bath that smelled of fresh-cut roses. She stepped into the bath and thought, *"This is so sweet! I can't believe that he remembered all of my favorites! I have to be sure to thank him."* Abbey soaked in the bath for about an hour before she decided it was time to get out. After she dried off, she applied the Versace body lotion and perfume. Then, she dressed and headed downstairs to find everyone sitting on the back patio sipping on pina coladas.

After spending a couple of hours relaxing and spending time with her friends, she looked at James and smiled.

"So, when do we get to meet Chuckalisa?" Abbey asked.

"Soon...Here shortly, I need to get ready. Are you Hoes coming to Chuckalisa's? Or are you going to stay here?" He asked.

"We are going with you!" the girls said at once.

"Then you, Hoes, need to go put something on that you can party in and put your faces on," he said, walking into the house.

Abbey, Ava, Hannah, and Sara followed James into the house and sprinted to their rooms to find dress boxes on each bed. The dresses were identical; they were black and form-fitting that hit mid-thigh. On the dress was a card with directions.

Ladies, you can style your hair and make-up any way you desire. The only thing I ask is to accent your eyes and lips. You will find shoes to match the dress in your shoe closet. Tonight will be so much fun to watch unfold.

~Cheers~

Chuckalisa Devine

The girls finished getting ready one by one, then waited in the living room for their host to join them. It wasn't long before they heard heels clicking on the tile. The sight of James left them in awe.

James was always taller than Abbey, but tonight...Chuckalisa wore the same dress as the girls and owned the black six-inch Christian Louboutin Red sole pumps. His hair was jet-black, which ended just above his heart-shaped ass. He had done a smokey eye in black and red, and his lips were Sin red. When he looked at the girls, they were stunned with their mouths open.

"Now, if you hoes are done catching flies. Get your asses up, and let's go," he said, smiling.

Chapter 4

ZayShawn~

As ZayShawn pushed the lock button on his key fob, he watched Brenna walk into Fetish with a new sub following close behind her. He scanned the parking lot and noticed everyone except James and Brad were there. It didn't matter what night of the week; Fetish was always full. Ready to relax and let the headache slip away, ZayShawn entered the club and took his usual spot at the far end of the bar, where he had a perfect view of the door.

"Here is your drink, Sir," the bartender said, setting down his drink.

"Thank you, Willow."

While ZayShawn sipped his Crown on the rocks, he watched Brenna work with her new sub in training. Her sub was a beautiful blonde; he could tell she had trouble submitting to a female. When the sub was bound to the St Andrews cross, Brenna looked up and locked eyes with ZayShawn. She whispered something to the sub and placed a blindfold over her eyes. Then Brenna crossed the room to ZayShawn.

"Do you have any plans tonight?" she asked.

"I have nothing planned," he smiled.

"Would you like a chance to put your training to the test?" she said with a wicked smile.

"What do you have in mind?"

"Well, I have this naughty sub that needs training. Plus, it will let me see how you are doing after graduation."

"What are her lessons for tonight?" he asked.

"She needs to learn how to submit to whoever she is screening with. She needs to learn the difference between pleasure and punishment."

"How new is she?"

"She is wet behind the ears. She knows a little about our world. A friend of mine asked if I would show her the ropes. She found curiosity about the BDSM world from reading books and wants to know if she has what it takes to live the lifestyle. Or it is just something she likes to read in books. This is my first night with her."

"What are your thoughts about her so far?" ZayShawn asked.

"She shows great potential; I think she is just struggling with submitting to a woman."

"I would be happy to help. I know I have found freedom in my training and lifestyle. I want to help others feel that freedom as well."

ZayShawn hoped it didn't show that his body quivered with anticipation. He tipped up the glass tumbler and drained the rest of the Crown. When he sat the tumbler down on the bar, the ice clinked against the sides. Brenna watched as her latest graduate confidently walked to the woman she had bound for him.

ZayShawn circled his sub for the night, deciding what he wanted to do first. Reaching over his head, he gripped the collar of his polo and pulled it off in one motion, exposing his chest for the first time in the club. His milk chocolate skin looked darker in the soft lighting.

He leaned down and said, "Don't move. Do you understand?"

"Yes..." she said quietly.

"You may call me Sir. Now, Mistress Raven told me you are having trouble following her directions. Is that true, Pet?"

"Yes..."

"Yes, what?"

"Yes, Sir."

"Good girl. That was a free one. I will add to your punishment every time you disrespect me by not using my title when you answer. Do you understand, Pet?"

"Yes."

Without hesitation, he swatted her hip, leaving a tiny sting behind.

"I'm sorry... I meant yes, Sir."

"The next one will be harder. Now I am going to unhook your cuffs from the cross. You may take off the blindfold. Next, you will undress; the only thing you will keep on is your panties. Then you will kneel at my feet and bow your head."

He watched as she looked around the club, trying to decide if she would obey his order. He mentally smiled when she closed her eyes, took a deep breath, and then started undressing. When she was done, she gracefully knelt at his feet, placing her hands on her thighs with her head bowed respectfully.

"Pet, as your Dom, I am responsible for correcting you when you have broken the rules. It is my pleasure to carry out your punishment and your pleasure. Do you agree with this?"

"Yes, Sir."

"Has Mistress Raven covered safe words with you?"

"Yes, Sir."

"Has she gone over how to answer your Dom properly?"

"Yes, Sir."

"Then why would you disrespect me?"

"I am sorry, Sir. I didn't mean to be disrespectful. I am nervous, and I forgot."

"Well, part of your training tonight will be punishment. This will help remind you always to respect your Dom."

"Only if it pleases you, Sir."

"Good Girl. Now stand and kiss your Master."

She rocked back on her heels and stood. ZayShawn fisted his hand in her hair and tipped her head back, controlling the kiss between them. When he broke the kiss between them, he turned her around to face the cross and fastened her wrists to the cuffs on the cross.

"I am going to enjoy watching your ivory skin turn pink," he growled as he cuffed her ankles to the cross.

When she was fully bound, he stood before the wall of whips and chose a leather flogger.

"Pet, I will warm up your skin before you are punished. Understand?"

"Yes, Sir."

"Good Girl, now don't move. Every time you flinch, it will add one more strike with the flogger."

"Yes, Sir."

ZayShawn swung the flogger next to her twice to help her relax. Then, when he was sure she would not move, he let the first blow land on the right cheek of her ass. Next, he placed the second one on the left, causing her to whimper.

"Color, Pet."

"Green, Sir."

"When we are screening, you may say colors only."

"Yes, Sir."

ZayShawn worked the flogger up and down her back, and when her skin was warmed, he said, "You will receive ten licks as your punishment. After you have received your punishment, I will reward you."

"Yes, Sir."

The next strike was more challenging, "Color, Pet."

"Yellow."

"Good, nine more, Pet."

Every time the flogger landed on her creamy pink skin, his cock jumped. When he gave the final blow, his cock was rock hard, and she was just on the edge of sub-space. ZayShawn laid the flogger on the table and released the sub from her bonds. She swayed a little when standing on her feet. ZayShawn swung her into his arms, carried her over to a couch, and laid her down. He turned to face the opening of the play space and watched as Mistress Raven pulled the curtain closed so they had privacy while he administered her aftercare. He picked her up and sat down, leaning her against him.

"You did wonderfully, Pet. Now relax and enjoy your reward."

She smiled shyly at him, "Thank you, Sir," she slurred, causing him to chuckle.

ZayShawn slid his hand inside her panties to find them soaking wet and very sensitive to his touch. He softly flicked her clit, making her arch her back and moan. She was so worked up from her first flogging it didn't take long for the blinding white orgasm to wash over her, causing her to scream. When her body stopped convulsing, he stood and rolled her onto her stomach. As she came down from her high, he rubbed cocoa butter balm into her pink skin to ensure no marks would mar her beautiful skin. When she started coming around, he said, "You did very well tonight. You have great potential to become a wonderful submissive. How did you feel about the session tonight?"

"Well, I was scared at first. Then, I was confused because my punishment aroused me. Then, I was happy because that was the biggest orgasm I had ever had."

"It is good that you are open to exploring your feelings. Also, talking to your Dom or Domme about your feelings when screening together is essential. It helps both of you to grow. I will give Misstress Raven an update on how you did tonight. Now I have a question for you. Why is it so hard for you to submit to Mistress Raven?"

"It bothers me because I am not gay," she said quietly.

"Look at it a different way. Look at it as pleasing your Master. Just because you are serving a Domme does not mean you are gay. You must learn all aspects of the lifestyle; the more you know, the more you can please your Dom when you find one. Put your trust in Mistress Raven; she only has your best interest at heart."

"I didn't think about that. I think I owe Misstress Raven an apology. May I please get dressed and rejoin my Mistress?" she asked.

"Yes, you may get dressed. But before you leave, clean the room with the disinfectant, and then, you may join us at the bar."

"Yes, Sir, and thank you for tonight."

~Abbey~

When the girls stepped outside James' house, a black stretch limo greeted them.

"Now, all you bitches don't get used to this. This is only for tonight to welcome you home. Now get the fuck in...the night is wasting away!" Chuckalisa snapped.

Sara and Hanna were the first to climb in; Ava and Abbey each kissed Chuckalisa on the cheek before crawling in next to the others. When Chuckalisa was in, she smiled at the new friends she had gained and said, "We are headed to Chuckalisa's."

"Yes, Ma'am." the driver answered.

"Now, my place is a little different. I hope you like it."

"What is it?" asked Ava.

"It is a chicken joint that is also an upscale strip club."

"Oh, Hannah, if you don't pass the bar, you can always shake your ass at Chuckalisa's," laughed Abbey.

"Fuck you, bitch," laughed Hannah.

"You dance?" asked Chuckalisa.

"Yes, I danced my way through law school. But, hey, I am debt free."

"You will find no judgment coming from me. You do what you need to do, boo," smiles Chuckalisa.

They laughed and sipped on champagne and watched as the nightlife came alive in Dallas. But Abbey focused on something else as they pulled up to Chuckalisa's. Her eyes never left the red neon sign that said Fetish. As the other girls entered his club, he noticed Abbey was in a trance. Chuckalisa looked at what her baby sister's eyes were locked on. She knew this could turn into a situation that he was uncomfortable about.

"Come on, sis; the others are waiting for us inside."

"Bubs...I mean, Chuckalisa, what is Fetish?"

"That is something you don't need to concern yourself with."

Chapter 5

Abbey~

When Abbey finally stepped inside Chuckalisa's, she was in pure awe. The restaurant was full of hungry people eating. From what Abbey read on the internet, Chuckalisa's Chicken Tits and Waffles was known for their chicken. You could find almost every type of chicken recipe there was. You could find the all-American favorite hamburger and fries at Chuckalisa's, but if you wanted something to write home about, you would order the special wings marinated in hot sauce for two days before dredging them into seasoned flour. You can find them on the menu named the Abbey Special.

Abbey watched as Chuckalisa was treated like royalty when walking through the dining room. Regular customers whooped and hollered as she walked through with a smile. She knocked twice when she reached a door with a sign that said VIP members only. When the door opened, Chuckalisa looked back at her entourage and said, "This way, Bitches!"

Chuckalisa had the VIP club dressed out in deep red and black silks. The booths were leather and crushed velvet.

"Oh...my...why did you choose such a deep red?" asked Sara

Chuckalisa looked back at her, and with a wicked smile, she said, "Sin, baby girl, red is the color of Sin."

"This place rocks!!" commented Hannah.

"Hoe, you must feel right at home," laughed Ava.

"Chuckalisa, the place looks amazing," Abbey said, turning in a circle, trying to take everything in.

"Thank you, little sister. Now you ladies, go sit down, and I will have someone come and take your orders. Your money is no good tonight. This is my treat to celebrate the first night of your new lives. Now I need to check on a few things. Sit, relax, and enjoy your night. I will be back after a while. You will find a table waiting for you. It is in the high-life section. That is the roped-off section over there," pointed Chuckalisa before walking off.

They walked in the direction they were told and found a selection of roped-off tables and a huge sign on one that said...*Reserved For Chuckalisa's Bitches!* Making them all laugh.

Abbey soaked in her surroundings while she and her best friends were treated like royalty. While sipping on some bubbly, she settled into the realization that this was real...This is now her new life...well, the start of her new life. She loved how James had bloomed into this beautiful person. He was every bit both people...by day; he was her brother James...But by night, Chuckalisa was the badass sister she had always wanted. She got the best of both worlds, no matter who he/she wanted to be.

The girls watched the exotic dancers as they danced. Chuckalisa had only the best dancers in her club. The club was crawling with men and women in business suits...They looked like they had powerful jobs. Sara pulled Abbey from her thoughts.

"You know...when we first walked into the club, I thought I would be uncomfortable here. But I'm not...this place is very welcoming."

"Right! Chuckalisa has one hell of a place. I am so proud of her. I know you weren't close to her when we were younger. I hope that will change. You both are amazing people," Abbey said, placing a hand on Sara's arm.

Before they knew it, they had a massive platter of wings on the table with a pitcher of Southern Sweet Tea.

"The boss said to eat up, and she will see you after the show," the server said before walking off.

The girls looked at each other, shrugged, and dug into the wings. Abbey fought tears as soon as she took a bite of the wings. She was eating her recipe. Without even knowing it, she had been here with James all along.

The first night she made the wings for James was when his dad threw him out of the house for being bi-sexual.

"Bitch, these wings are fire," Ava said as she shoved another wing into her mouth.

"I know, right," Hannah chirped.

They watched the club's atmosphere change as they ate and guzzled tea. They all went still when the music stopped, and Chuckalisa's voice announced the show's start.

"Ladies and Gentlemen...Tonight we are doing something a little different to welcome my sister and my girls home. My drag daughters and I are going to put on a little show. So sit back and relax, and don't forget about handing out them dollar bills, baby. Enjoy!"

The MC quickly took back the mic and introduced Chuckalisa herself with a message to Abbey.

"Abbey, this song is for you...Just know I am happy and healthy. Now that you and the girls are here, I need just one last thing, and my life will be complete. This song says it all...Commitment by Monica."

They watched as Chuckalisa worked the stage and the crowd. As she sang, she put the crowd in a trance. When the song was done, the crowd showered her with money.

When she left the stage, the MC introduced the next performer.

"The next gem here to perform for you tonight...Is Blue Diamond with Tina Turner's Private Dancer."

Blue Diamond was a beautiful black woman with sea-green eyes. She was wearing a red one-piece catsuit with stilettos to match. They watched as she danced and sang, and the stage slowly filled with one-dollar bills. When she finished collecting her tips, the MC announced the next.

"Whoo...Didn't she shine? Now let's give a warm welcome to our next beautiful flower. I give you Sunset Rose performing S & M by Rihanna."

Sunset Rose was a raven beauty with blue eyes. She wore a black and blue corset, leather shorts with blue fishnet stockings, black knee-high boots, and a bullwhip coiled in her hand. She would snap every so often, and to tie it all together, she had handcuffs hooked to the loops in her leather shorts. Sunset Rose had the men eating out of her palm. When she was done, the MC announced the last performer of the night.

"Now, last but not least, I give you the light in the dark...Here is Midnight Star. She will perform Unstoppable by Sia."

Midnight Star was a drop-dead beauty. She had perfect curls that hung loosely past her waist. She wore a wide neck cut tee shirt that hung off one shoulder, daisy duke jean shorts with black heels. When Midnight Star did three backflips and landed on her feet every time, Sara slid off the seat and said, "Um, that bitch is not human."

"Agreed," the others said in unison.

When the show was done, they met with Chuckalisa behind the stage.

"Well, ladies, did you enjoy yourselves?" asked Chuckalisa.

"Yes, thank you for such a wonderful welcome," Sara said.

"I had a blast," squealed Hannah as she hugged Chuckalisa.

"Bitch, this has been the best night of my life so far," Ava said, kissing her cheek.

"Sister, this was amazing. I am so proud of you," Abbey said, leaning into Chuckalisa and putting an arm around her.

"I am glad. The limo is outside waiting to take you home so you can get some sleep," said Chuckalisa.

"Oh. You're not coming?" Abbey asked.

"I have something I need to take care of. I will be home in the morning for coffee and a little breaky," she said, kissing Abbey's head.

"Ok. We will see you at home. Thank you again for tonight. I love you," said Abbey.

"Yea, yea...see you bitches at home. Love ya too."

When they were getting ready to get into the limo, Abbey noticed Chuckalisa had exited the club and was walking down to Fetish.

"Hey...hold on a minute. Come on, guys, let's follow her. She was acting weird earlier tonight when I asked about that place. Now she is going in there. I want to know what it is, and I want to know what she is up to," Abbey said, looking at the others.

The others were just as curious as Abbey, so they told the limo to wait there, and they would be back. Abbey's stomach had butterflies, like when she would sneak out at night to hang out with James. Abbey gripped the gold door handle, took a deep breath and pulled the door open, and walked in. The girls were stunned at what they found.

Chapter 6

ZayShawn

As Zayshawn sat at the bar unwinding from his first scene since graduation, he wondered to himself if he would ever find his sub. Then he hears a commotion coming from the front of the club. He looked up to see that one of the club's most sought-after and respected dommes had walked into the club, Chuckalisa Devine. ZayShawn noticed she had looked his way, so he held up his glass in salute to her as she passed him. He quickly returned to his thoughts, beginning to feel loneliness set in when his mind told him to look up at the door.

He looked up just in time to see four women walk in that clearly did not belong there as they looked so out of place in their clubbing attire. That is when he spotted her and could not take his eyes off her. From the first sight of that beautiful blue hair, he knew she would be the one. Just then, he heard Chuckalisa, from a few seats away, say, "Damn it! I knew I couldn't leave those bitches unattended!"

ZayShawn watched as Chuckalisa made her way over to the girls. He made his way closer so that he could hear the conversation clearer.

"Abbey, I thought I told you to go home and get some rest."

"C'mon, sis, the night is still young! We didn't want to just go home!" whined Abbey.

"Yea!" echoed Ava.

"This is not the place for you girls to be. Trust me when I tell you that you are NOT ready for this."

Sara stood frozen, looking around. Clearly, the other girls had not taken a moment to look at what they truly walked into. Sara's eyes grew wider, and her jaw dropped the more she looked. She nudged Hannah with her elbow. Hannah began to truly look and got a huge smile across her face. At that moment, Abbey and Ava took their attention off of Chuckalisa and noticed their surroundings as well, both getting a look of intrigue across their faces.

"Oh, no no no. You are NOT staying!!" said Chuckalisa.

"Oh yes, we are!" yelled Ava, Abbey, and Hannah while Sara stood there drop-jawed and unable to speak.

"Either we come here with you, or we come alone! Your choice!" said Ava.

ZayShawn stood just far enough away that he could hear the conversation, mesmerized by the blue-haired beauty. Her eyes matched her hair, and that smile lit up the entire club. Could this be her? Could this woman that he had never even met be the one? She seemed a bit headstrong. Could he actually tame her?

"Ugh, I guess it's better that you are here with me. That way, you are under my protection. C'mon bitches." sighed Chuckalisa as she led them through the club to the bar. Sara stood rooted to the spot until Hannah grabbed her by the arm and pulled her along. "Let's go scary."

ZayShawn, feeling somewhat like a stalker, couldn't help but follow the blue-haired beauty while also trying to hurry back to his spot at the bar before they could pass by, hoping his friend would stop to introduce him to her friends.

Abbey

When the girls entered the establishment that they watched their friend disappear into, it was dark, and their eyes needed to adjust to the light after being outside under all the neon, despite the fact that it was nighttime.

Just as Abbey's eyes adjusted in the new lighting, she heard Chuckalisa's voice reprimanding them. Amid her tirade about them not being there, she looked around and noticed that they were definitely overdressed compared to every other woman in attendance. At first glance, it seemed like any other upscale nightclub, but after looking closer, it was nothing at all what it seemed. The space was a warehouse turned into a club. There were couches in all surrounding open rooms with different "stages" set up. Each "stage" contained different apparatuses. Some looked like torture devices, while others just looked like regular house furniture at first glance.

When Chuckalisa finally let them stay, she led them across the room to the bar. That's when Abbey spotted him. He was tall, milk chocolate-skinned, with soft light brown eyes, supple lips, waist-length dreadlocks, and a very slim build. Abbey felt as if she needed to wipe the drool from her lip.

Just as they were approaching him, Chuckalisa stopped and spoke to her friend. "Zayshawn Williams, these are my girls from back home. Abbey, Ava, Sara, and Hannah."

ZayShawn took Abbey's hand and gently placed a kiss on her knuckles. "It is so very nice to meet you, Abbey. Can I offer you a drink?"

Abbey blushed and replied, "Sure."

"What do you drink?"

"Crown Apple and Sprite,"

"A woman after my heart," he said, smiling. "And your friends?"

Abbey had almost forgotten that her friends were even there for a second. She looked back at them and asked them what they wanted.

Hannah wanted a white wine, Sara, a Blue Maui, and Ava, a Long Island Iced Tea.

Abbey relayed the drink order to ZayShawn, and he placed the order. Abbey couldn't take her eyes off the man in front of her. She barely heard Chuckalisa speak when she asked ZayShawn to keep an eye on the girls while she went to handle some business, giving him a look that he totally understood.

While they stood there waiting for their drinks, the girls were all looking around the club, taking in all the scenery. Hannah, Ava, and Abbey looked around as so many questions came into their minds. Sara was busy biting her lip, looking like a deer in headlights, not knowing what to think. When their drinks arrived, ZayShawn handed each drink to the girls, saving Abbey for last. "Here you are, beautiful," he said, letting their fingers brush. Abbey blushed and said, "Thank you, ZayShawn."

ZayShawn smiled, and Abbey nearly melted into a puddle at his feet. Abbey couldn't believe this man was having this kind of effect on her. No man had ever made her feel this way just from his presence. All she knew was that she HAD to get to know him more, and she would make Chuckalisa tell her all she wanted to know if she had to.

The group stood at the bar a little while longer. Finally, ZayShawn offered for them to all have a more comfortable seat on one of the oversized couches in front of the stage Chuckalisa would be performing. The girls agreed, and ZayShawn led them across the room with his hand placed on the small of Abbey's back. Once they were all seated, ZayShawn took his seat next to Abbey.

"So, Abbey, what brings you to Dallas?" ZayShawn asked.

"After graduation, I got a call from my childhood best friend telling me to come to Dallas. So, I called the girls, packed all of my stuff, and got a Uhaul. And here I am, sitting with you and having a drink."

"So, you decided to make a big move. But why?"

"Honestly, ZayShawn, I feel like I have outgrown Middlesboro. The only family that I have left is here with me now, and I missed my best friend so much. James, I'm sorry; Chuckalisa is the closest thing to a sibling that I have ever had. I grew up an only child, and I lost both of my parents." Abbey explained, looking at her lap.

"I am so sorry to hear that," said ZayShawn. "Maybe after tonight, you will have more family."

Abbey looked up into his eyes and smiled.

"Let me get you another drink," Zayshawn said as he waved over a scantily clad waitress. ZayShawn ordered another drink for each of them.

As they waited for their drinks, Abbey craved to continue her conversation with ZayShawn.

"So, ZayShawn, are you originally from Dallas?" asked Abbey.

"Yes, ma'am. Born and raised. My father raised me and my two brothers after our mom passed," he said.

"I am so sorry to hear that."

"Thank you. I barely remember her. I was only two when she passed away from cancer. My brothers remember her more than I do. Although I have had an amazing mother figure. My dad has been with his girlfriend Faye since I was about five years old."

"Well, I am so happy to know that. Everyone needs that in their life."

The waitress returned and handed fresh drinks to Ava, Hannah, and Sara. ZayShawn took Abbey's glass and handed it to her. Just as Abbey turned to continue her conversation with ZayShawn, the curtain in front of her opened up, and when she looked up, her jaw dropped almost to the floor. She nudged Ava, who was sitting next to her, and heard a loud gasp from all the girls sitting to her right.

When they looked up, they saw their friend, Chuckalisa Devine, dressed in full red leather. Chuckalisa had her raven black hair pulled into a tight, fierce ponytail that brushed her exposed ass cheeks.

The conversation between Abbey and ZayShawn was lost, and the girls found it very hard to speak when they fully looked at the scene that was about to unfold. Chuckalisa had two subs bowed at her feet. The male had light mocha-colored skin and was muscular; his hair was in braids and pulled up in a tight bun to make it safe for play. The female had flawless porcelain white skin and dark chestnut brown hair done up in a French braid. They both were wearing nothing but black thongs. Sara was the first to find her voice.

"Umm...umm...What is she going to do to them?"

"She is going to play with them and give them pleasure," said ZayShawn, leaning back on the couch and placing his arms across the back in hopes Abbey would lean into him.

They watched as Chuckalisa circled her subs, deciding on what she wanted to do.

"I think I will call you Pearl because of your beautiful skin," she said to the female. "And what to call you, my little Mocha delight? I think I will call you Pet because your skin reminds me of a Mocha Bunny at Easter," she said to the male.

Abbey leaned back into ZayShawn and asked softly, "Why is she calling them different names? Why doesn't she use their real names?"

ZayShawn leaned toward Abbey. He was so close she could feel his breath on her ear and said, "When a Dom or a Domme scenes with a sub, they use pet names just as a sub would call a Dom or Domme by their preferred name. It is done out of respect for the DS community."

"DS community?" she asked.

"DS stands for Dominate and Submissive; some call it S&M, which is Slave and Master. I take it you know little about the lifestyle?"

"I know nothing. But what I have seen has been very enticing," she blushed.

"I would love to talk to you more and get your thoughts about my lifestyle. So sit back like a good girl and watch the show, then we can talk about what you thought about it," he commanded softly.

Abbey heard the command in his voice; she was a little confused about why her belly quivered and why her pussy jumped at being told what to do. She has always been a very independent woman. She decided she would figure that out later. Now, she was going to watch her sister work her magic.

~ZayShawn~

ZayShawn kept a close eye on Abbey, Ava, Hannah, and Sara, ensuring nothing from Chuckalisa's scene would cause negative triggers. Chuckalisa bound each sub to the suspension bar, giving them little room to move. Chuckalisa chose a riding crop for her first prop. She randomly flicked the crop's tip across their bodies as she circled her subs. Abbey let out a slight moan when Chuckalisa snapped the crop on Pearl's hard nipples, then again when she connected with her clit through her thong. When she connected with her ass, it left her skin pink, and every time the crop connected with her ass, it jiggled.

"Color my pretty pink Pearl," she asked.

"Green, Master."

"Good girl," she praised.

Chuckalisa approached her other sub and said, "You have been such a good boy waiting your turn. Would you like to wear my marks, Pet?"

"Yes, Master," he answered.

"What stripes would you like, Pet? Do you want the cat o nine, or would you like the bite of the bull?" she asked.

"Whatever pleases you, Master, would be my pleasure to wear," he answered.

Chuckalisa smiled at her sub and kissed him on the cheek before walking over to the wall and picking up the seven-foot bullwhip. It was crafted with red and black braided leather. Chuckalisa cracked the whip a few times, making her sub shiver with anticipation.

"The first couple of licks of my whip will be just a whisper of a kiss on your skin. Then, after your skin is nice and warm, I will let you wear my marks. If you are a good boy, I will reward you. Do you understand, Pet?" she asked.

"Yes, Mistress...I mean Master."

"Pet, you may call me Misstress if you wish."

"Thank you, Mistress," he purred.

ZayShawn watched Abbey's reaction to the bullwhip, knowing it was his favorite. When the first strike landed on the subs' back, he noticed Abbey had squirmed in her seat. When the first testing blow landed on the sub, Abbey moaned along with the sub, making ZayShawn smile.

Abbey watched in awe as the person she had known her whole life created angel wings with the marks left behind on the sub's back.

"Omg...that is beautiful," she whispered.

"Chuckalisa is one of our community's most trusted Dommes and the most wanted. How she has stayed so long without collaring a sub is beyond me. She has many talents, one of her specialties is the bullwhip. Hopefully, you will see the other tonight as well," ZayShawn said softly.

Chuckalisa was panting from the sexual tension building between her and her subs. She dropped the whip and stood in front of her sub.

"You were a very good boy. You have made your Mistress very happy. Are you ready for your reward pet?" she asked.

"Yes, Mistress."

Chuckalisa gripped him by the throat and kissed him. The sub whined in disappointment when she broke the kiss, making Chuckalisa chuckle.

"Don't worry, Pet, that wasn't your treat. I took that kiss because I wanted to. When I release you from your bonds, I want you to ready the table for Pearl," she commanded.

"Yes, Mistress."

When the sub was released from his bonds, Chuckalisa rubbed his wrists and arms to help restore circulation. The sub quickly pulled the table into the center of the stage and began hooking cuffs on each leg of the table. When she unbound the other sub, she rubbed her wrists and arms. She could see the fear in Pearl's eyes because of the trauma that was done to her by her last Master. Chuckalisa softly kissed her and said, "There is no need for fear, my beautiful pink Pearl. I am not a monster like your previous Master. Remember, you have a safe word if you are uncomfortable about anything. But I promise you will enjoy everything."

She nodded and gave a small smile. Then she stood beside the table, waiting for her instructions.

"Climb on the table, Pearl, and lay down."

Chuckalisa and her sub quickly bound her to the table, and with one quick pull, she broke the side string of her thong and removed it, leaving her bare.

Chuckalisa looked at her sub and said, "Pet, you may fuck her, but do it gently, make sure she feels every inch of your big cock with every stroke."

"Yes, Mistress."

Her sub quickly removed his thong and stood between her legs. With one slow, torturous stroke, he sank balls deep into Pearl's wet pussy. He filled her to almost bursting when he bottomed out; she screamed in ecstasy, arching her back. As he fucked her slowly, Chuckalisa moved around the stage, gathering the props she needed.

Chuckalisa stood behind the table and placed a glass of clear liquid down; she took metal tongs with a cotton ball and dipped it in the liquid. She picked up another cotton ball with another set of tongs and placed it in the liquid. She pulled one tong out of the glass and set it on fire. With the wet one, she traced her nipples, making them wet. She placed it back in the glass and then touched the fire to her nipple, setting the liquid to dance with flames. Just as quick as she lit it, she patted out the fire so it left behind only the heat, making Pearl moan. Chuckalisa did this a couple more times, drawing patterns on Pearl and putting on a fire show. When she was done, Chuckalisa put the flaming cotton ball in a glass of water and placed the props on the floor. She moved over to the head of the table and bent to kiss Pearl.

"Pearl, you have done very well. Now I want you to tip your head back and open your mouth. My pet and I are going to give you the fucking of your dreams. This is your reward, my beautiful pink Pearl."

When ZayShawn looked at Abbey, her eyes were as big as dinner plates, and her mouth hung to her knees. She gasped and moved to the edge of her seat when Chuckalisa pulled out his cock and face, fucked Pearl while telling her sub to move faster and to go deeper.

"Fuck her, Pet! Make her see stars."

Chuckalisa held the sides of Pearl's face as she pumped in and out of her throat.

"Cum now, my pets," she growled.

After all three of them found their release, he slowly pulled his cock out of her mouth and pulled his pants back up. Chuckalisa's Pet pulled out of Pearl and unbound her legs. When she was freed from her bonds, Chuckalisa picked her up and cradled her in her arms. She nodded to ZayShawn, letting him know the curtains could be closed, so he signaled to the bouncer, and they pulled it shut to give her privacy to give her aftercare.

ZayShawn looked over at Abbey as the curtains closed, trying to gauge her reactions and read her thoughts. "So, what did you think?"

"That was like nothing I have ever seen."

"Oh, I am sure. But what are your thoughts on it?" he probed.

"I'm not sure. It looked like they both really enjoyed themselves. But it looked like it would hurt. How can that feel good?" Abbey said. "And to call someone 'Master' or 'Mistress,' I just don't get that part."

"Well, I can tell you that while it LOOKS painful, it definitely is not. There is a lot of pleasure in the pain."

"You sound like you speak from experience," said Abbey.

ZayShawn wasn't sure if he should divulge the information to Abbey that he was a Dom himself just yet, but how else was he supposed to explain to her he, in fact, was speaking from experience? ZayShawn decided quickly that he might as well tell her.

"Well, in order to become a true and fair Dom, one has to first become a sub. That is the only way that one can truly understand the true dynamics." ZayShawn held his breath as he waited for Abbey's response. He watched her as the realization sunk into her mind.

"Yup, I just lost her. She's going to run." he thought to himself.

"So, let me get this straight. You are a Dom?" she asked. "And you used to be a sub?"

"Yes, I am a Dom, but no, I didn't use to be a sub. I went through Dominant training, and in that training, I had to be submissive to understand what my sub will go through fully," he explained.

As she thought about what he said, ZayShawn was nervous about what her response would be.

"I think I get it. It actually makes sense—all except the training. Is there actually a training course that you have to go through? Like a school?" was her response.

ZayShawn chuckled. "Not every Dom goes through training. But the best Doms do. There are a lot of self-proclaimed Doms that truly do not understand what it means. I would love to get together with you and maybe answer questions you may have."

Abbey looked up into his light brown eyes and smiled that smile that melted him in his seat. "ZayShawn, I would love that."

Chapter 7

James interrupted Abbey and ZayShawn's conversation.

"Let's go, ladies. I am taking you home because none of you can do what you are told," James growled.

"Abbey, may I have your phone number?" asked ZayShawn.

"That would be a NO!" he said to ZayShawn, never taking his eyes off Abbey. "I said it is time to go. Now move your asses," James growled and pointed at the door.

Sara was the first to beat feet and headed to the door. When all the girls were safely outside the club, James turned and looked at ZayShawn.

"What gives you the right to ask my little sister for her number? You need a sub. As a matter of fact, this lifestyle is not for Abbey or any of these girls," James said as he crossed his arms.

"No disrespect...but that decision should be up to her," ZayShawn said carefully.

"Let me talk to her first. This was a shock to her system. We come from a tiny bum-fucked-town. In our old town, you would be shunned if you were from the LGBTQ+ community. My father kicked me out of the house on my seventeenth birthday because he found out that I was Bi-sexual. Abbey and her friends were the only ones that still treated me like a human; the rest of the town treated me like I had leprosy. So please do me this favor. Let me talk to her first, and if she is okay with stepping into our world, I will give her your number."

"James, I am going to tell it to you straight. I like her. I like her a lot. I want to see where this could go with her, but I will respect you if you both say no."

James nodded and left the club to take his bratty girls home. When James exited the club, the girls were nowhere to be seen. He found them sitting quietly in the limo. When he sat down, he looked at the girls and then looked out the window, trying to rein in his anger before speaking. Abbey was the first to speak.

"Bubbs..."

"Not yet, Abbey...Let me get my head together, then we can talk," James said quietly.

The ride home was quiet. When they pulled into his drive, he said, "Ladies, I love you all, and we can talk about what you saw tonight in the morning. Please give me tonight to talk to my sister," asked James.

"Night," was all Sara said before running inside.

"Thank you for tonight, James. I had a blast," Hannah said before following Sara.

"Goodnight, James," Ava said, kissing his cheek, then whispering, "You are a bad bitch. If you feel embarrassed for us seeing the real you. I will beat your ass. Good Night, Love."

"Bubbs," Abbey tried one more time.

"Abbey, my love, we can talk, but can we please talk inside where I can have a drink?" he asked.

Saying nothing, Abbey smiled and grabbed his hand, and pulled him toward the house.

When they were inside, James led Abbey to his sitting quarters to talk, just the two of them. Abbey kicked off her shoes and curled up on the couch, waiting for James to sit down. She watched him pour himself a peanut butter whiskey over some ice in a short glass; after taking a sip, he joined Abbey on the couch.

"I am so damn mad at you I can hardly see straight. If you were mine, I would have already paddled your ass so you couldn't sit down for a week," he said softly.

"James, what the hell do you mean by that? Plus, you have no right to be mad at me. We don't have secrets. You are just mad because I saw the other side of who you are," pouted Abbey.

"Wrong! I am pissed because you put yourself and the other girls in danger."

"How?"

"Abbey, you and the girls walked into a FUCKING BDSM sex club alone. None of you were wearing protection collars. Not all Doms are safe like me. There are some sick men out there that get pleasure out of torturing women. I would have told you about this side of me soon. I just needed to figure out how to keep you safe. I told you a long time ago, you are my entire world. If anything ever happened to you, it would kill me. You are my family, Abbs," James explained.

"I'm sorry, Bubs. But I am glad I went. Now I know who you are, inside and out. And I love every piece of you. I am in awe of you. How did you get into this lifestyle?" she asked.

"Well, when I first moved down here, I needed a job, and the first person who gave me a chance was LaMarkus Williams. He gave me a job as a bartender. My first night in Fetish was an eye-opener. I felt at home within the community, plus they accepted me...all of me. For the first time, I didn't need to hide my sexuality. So I asked him about the lifestyle, and between him and his friend Brenna, they helped me bloom into who I am today. I quickly learned that I was not submissive. But make one hell of a Dom/Domme," he said, smiling.

"You said his last name was Williams. ZayShawn's last name is Williams. Are they related?"

"Sister, LaMarkus is ZayShawn's father. They own Fetish."

"Is ZayShawn a respectful Dom?"

"ZayShawn is a good man, and I believe he will be a respectful Dom."

"He told me he was a Dom already. Did he lie?"

"No, He is just a new Dom. The same Domme taught us. So, in time, yes, he will become a respectful Dom. Before we get into this conversation, I need to ask you a few questions."

"Okay."

"From what you have seen, how do you feel?"

"I am confused, excited, intrigued, curious, and sexually frustrated. Who knew watching my brother whip, play, and fuck two subs at once would make me wet? Sorry if that sounded creepy."

"No, on my side, that doesn't sound creepy. The way I see it...the scene sexually turned you on, not who was performing it. Now I am going to pry some answers out of you. I am not asking as your brother...I am asking you as a Dom. You really need to make sure you are ready for this. If you want to dabble in this lifestyle, we need to ensure you understand what you are stepping into. What excited you the most? Can you handle being under the control of another? Abbey, I know your past. You are brilliant, rebellious, strong-willed, and thick-headed. Can you truly submit to someone else? The true meaning of submission is...the condition of being submissive, humble, or compliant: an act of submitting to the authority or control of another."

"Well, when you put it that way...You make it sound scary. Are you trying to scare me?" she asked.

"I asked you some questions, and you still have not answered them. Do you need to be taught a lesson?"

"What the fuck? Who the hell do you think you are talking to me like that?" Abbey huffed.

Saying nothing, James grabbed Abbey's arm and pulled her over his knee. He placed one hand on her back and lifted her dress with the other. Then he landed three hard smacks on her ass. He pulled her dress down and sat her back on the couch.

"That was for disobeying. Now answer the questions I asked you, then you can ask yours."

Angry tears filled her eyes, and she sat quietly, trying to figure out if she wanted to punch him for putting his hands on her or comply by answering his questions. Knowing nothing in this world would make him hurt her, so she sighed and slumped on the couch.

"First Dick Face, all of it excited me. The bondage and the bullwhip were the best. Second, with time and understanding of the rules, yes. I could give my submission," Abbey said, pouting.

"You get that one for free. When we are in the club and around others in our community, you will not disrespect me as a Dom by calling me anything other than my title. What questions do you have? Now is the time to ask."

"Does this mean I will lose my brother if I step into this lifestyle?"

"No, I will always be your brother. I am just trying to make you see this lifestyle is not for everyone. We must stay true to our roles if we are around other people from our community. If we are home or just being us, we are the same James and Abbey we have always been. What is your next question?"

"Why did you put your hands on me?" she asked with a sniffle.

"I corrected you for disobeying a command," he said gently.

"Oh. If I step into the lifestyle, will I be giving myself up?" she asked quietly.

"What do you mean?"

"Will I be giving away my free will?"

"No. When you become a submissive, you agree to give yourself over to your Dom and entrust him to take care of you. You will still make all your own decisions. Still, live your life with minor tweaks that make things so much yummier."

"I think I understand," Abbey said, letting out a deep breath.

"So...The question is...Do you still want to step into the lifestyle?"

"I want to test the waters and see if it is for me."

James sighed and shook his head, knowing he couldn't change her mind. "Okay, but I have rules you will follow. Not because I want to control you, it is to keep you safe. I want you to wear a protective collar now that they will see you in our community. I will give you ZayShawn's number; you can contact him if you choose. But you will always need to keep that collar on, whether you are in or out of the club. Understood?"

"But if I wear your collar, how can I be with ZayShawn?"

"It is not my collar...It will keep other Doms from approaching you. I will let ZayShawn know you will wear a protection collar for your safety. Then, if you choose to be in the lifestyle and he collars you, I will remove the protection. If you don't agree, I will do everything in my power to stop you from entering that club ever again. Do we have a deal?"

"Because you know about this kind of thing...yes, we have a deal."

"Okay, good. Now I think it is best if we all get some sleep. I will see you in the morning. I love you, baby girl."

Abbey stood and hugged James. "I love you too, big brother."

Abbey walked to the door and looked back at her brother; he was slumped back on the couch with his head tipped back and an arm over his eyes. Deciding not to disturb him, she shut his door and went down the hall to Ava's room. She found her light was off, and Ava was fast asleep; she looked at her watch and noticed it was almost four am. So she decided she needed some sleep as well. When she entered her room, she kicked the door shut, fell face-first onto the bed and was out in seconds.

~The Dream~

Abbey stood just inside the doors of Fetish, looking for a place to sit. She was wearing a corset that was royal blue and black. The tips of the ribbons that tied it shut brushed the top of her heart-shaped ass. Her skirt stopped just below the swell of her ass. She wore stockings with a seam that ran up the back of her legs and, to tie the whole outfit together, her pumps were black with a royal blue stole. Abbey wore her hair in an upside-down French braid, curls spilling around her face.

She sat on the couch at the far end of the room and waited for a server to take her order. When the server approached her, he handed her a drink and said, "Here you go, Miss Abbey."

"What is this?" she asked.

"It is a crown apple and sprite, ma'am."

"How did you know what I wanted to drink?"

"Because I ordered it for you. Now thank him and enjoy your drink," said the voice that made her weak in the knees.

"Thank you," she said while lifting the glass to her lips.

Without asking, ZayShawn sat down on the other end of the couch and turned to face Abbey.

"I am glad you called," he said with cock sure grin. "So, my dear, what did you have in mind? Did you want to talk, or do you want to play?"

"I am scared to death to tell you this, but...I want to play," she said, blushing.

ZayShawn stood and held out his hand. "Then come with me, my pretty little pet."

Abbey looked into his eyes and tipped up her glass, downing the rest of her drink. When she placed her hand in his, the butterflies in her stomach started flittering. He led her to the stage that Chuckalisa used and said, "Kneel and wait for me to set up the scene."

Abbey knelt on the mat and watched ZayShawn move around the stage. When he grabbed the black leather cuffs, she quivered. ZayShawn approached her and said, "Hold out your wrists, pet."

Abbey held her wrist out to him and asked, "What would you like me to call you?"

"Tonight, you will call me Master. If you want to stop a scene, you need to say stop. When you answer me, you will only say yes, Master, or no, Master."

"Yes, Master."

"Good girl."

"Now stand and serve your master."

Abbey stood and waited for his next command. ZayShawn took her by the hand and led her to the suspension bar. He turned and looked at her as he clipped the cuffs to the bar.

"You look quite beautiful, all bound up, ready for me to play with. I love the outfit you are wearing. But it will look much better off. What made you wear this tonight?"

"I didn't want to stand out."

When ZayShawn unlaced her corset, she started moving to shy away.

"No need for you to shy away. You are beautiful," he soothed.

After ZayShawn removed her clothing, he softly leaned in and kissed her shoulder.

"You are so beautiful," he said softly.

She instantly missed his touch when he moved over to the wall of whips, canes, floggers, and paddles. She watched him choose a leather and fleece double-sided paddle.

"Pet, I want to paddle that pretty ass of yours and turn it a lovely shade of pink. If it becomes too much for you to handle, say stop."

"Yes, Master."

ZayShawn started by rubbing the fleece side of the paddle so she would relax and not pull on the restraints. When she was relaxed, he spoke softly in her ear, "You will now receive five swats with my paddle. If you are a good girl, I will reward you."

Just as she was about to receive the first swat, the sound of knocking on her door pulled her from the dream.

Chapter 8

Abbey~

"BITCH...GO AWAY!"

"Wake the fuck up," Ava said, opening the door.

"I said...go away! You sure know how to fuck up a wet dream," grumbled Abbey.

"What are you talking about?" Ava asked as she climbed onto the bed.

"I was having the best dream until your ass knocked on my door."

"Oh, yeah...What was it about?" asked Ava, wiggling her eyebrows.

"I was in Fetish with ZayShawn, and he had me all cuffed and bound. Just as he was about to spank me, you friggen knocked," Abbey pouted.

"Ohhh...sorry," Ava apologized.

"Oh, well...So why were you beating on my door at 7 am?" Abbey asked as she sat up in bed.

"I wanted to talk to you about last night...you know, the club," said a giddy Ava.

"Yea, what about it?" Abbey asked.

"What did you think about it?"

"Well, considering the dream I was having, I am intrigued by the lifestyle," Abbey answered.

"I am too. But where do we start? How do we learn about the lifestyle? Who do we ask?"

"Well, James would be an excellent place to start. We talked last night, and it was a good talk. James wants me to wear a protection collar."

"Why?"

"James said there are a lot of Doms and Dommes that don't know what they are doing. The protection collar will keep them away from me. Plus, he gave me ZayShawn's phone number last night."

"Oh...Well, that makes it a little scary to step into the lifestyle. Are you going to call him?"

"I am thinking about it. We need to tell James that you are also interested in the lifestyle. That way, if you have questions, you can ask him," suggested Abbey.

"I know we are becoming friends, but do you think he will talk to me about the lifestyle?" she asked.

"Yes, I know he will, and I can give you three reasons. One, you and James are becoming friends. Two, he is a respectful Dom. Three, James is a lovely person inside and out," Abbey said, smiling.

"I am scared to talk to him. I don't know him that well, Abbey. Plus, this conversation will head to the discussion of sex...really kinky sex."

"Yes, it will; we talked last night, and it opened my eyes. Trust me, talk to him. If you are going to be scared like Sara, I will go with you. Now get the fuck out and let me try to finish my dream," Abbey said, laying back down and pulling the covers over her head.

Abbey threw the covers off a few hours later and stomped to the bathroom to shower. Cussing Ava the whole way; *I need to smack that bitch. Pounding on my door at o' dark hundred hours and pulling me out of what was going to be the best sex dream of my life. Just wait; that bitch will get what's coming to her.*

When she finished getting dressed, she padded downstairs and found everyone eating breakfast at the breakfast bar.

"Well, good morning, sleepyhead," James greeted with a smile.

After greeting her brother with a kiss, she sat down across from Ava and smiled sweetly at her best friend.

"Please pass the coffee," she asked Ava, never letting her smile falter.

"Sure," said Ava.

As Abbey fixed her cup of coffee, James set a plate in front of her. Abbey was going to get her revenge on Ava. She just needed to wait until the timing was right. When everyone was eating and discussing their plans, Abbey waited for the right time to strike. When it got quiet, Abbey went in for the kill.

"Hey, Bubs, Ava wants to talk to you about the BDSM lifestyle. She is too chicken to tell you herself. Oh, and can you please pass the butter?"

"You are a fucking bitch, Abbey," yelled Ava.

"Wait, what the hell did I miss?" asked Hannah.

"This bitch wants to act like Sara, a scary bitch," Abbey shot back.

"What the hell did I do?" asked Sara.

James watched as the girls yelled back and forth. When Abbey picked up a serving spoon and chucked it at Ava's head, he stepped in.

Abbey watched the change takeover James as he stepped into his dominant role.

"That is about enough," he growled while standing. "I will have none of you acting like uncivilized brats in my house. If you are going to play like you want to live in this lifestyle, you all will be treated as such."

"But no one said..." Sara stammered.

"I said quiet. When I am in this role, you all will be respectful and follow the rules. The first rule is that you are all friends. You will not treat each other with disrespect. If you do, you will be punished. Two, Abbey, you need to apologize to Ava. She is just like you and knows nothing about the lifestyle."

"Fuck that..."

"Abbey, that's one," growled James.

"James, she fucking started it," yelled Abbey.

"Abbey," he said, holding up two fingers.

"How is this my fault, hoe bag? You are the one that opened your fucking mouth," spit Ava.

"Ava, that is enough if. I am telling you, if you keep going, you will be punished," James warned.

"I still don't know how it is my fault, and two, you're not man enough to tame me," yelled Ava.

Abbey's eyes went huge, and she shook her head at Ava. "Umm. Ava, I would quit while you are ahead."

"Bitch, for the last time, shut the fuck up. I am a big girl, and I can take care of things myself," she huffed.

James untied his robe, pulled the belt from the loops, and stalked to Ava, quickly binding her. He reached above the breakfast bar, pulling a suspension bar into place and securing her to it. The others watched as he pushed a button on the wall, and a hidden door swung open. He took out a paddle that said, BAD GIRL. When he returned to Ava, he moved her robe away from her ass and gave her five good smacks. She had a lonely tear sliding down her cheek when he looked at her.

"Are you ready to be a good girl?"

Without saying a word, she nodded.

"Now, I know you are confused as to why this happened. If you can act like you have some brains in your head, we will all sit down and talk about what happened here this morning," he said softly.

He unbound Ava, and she sat quietly, waiting to see what would happen next. They watched as James approached Abbey and said, "Bend over the stool."

Abbey did not want to cross him again after what happened last night, so she submitted to a Dom for the first time in her life. Abbey bent over the stool and proudly took her two whacks.

Everyone was quiet while they finished eating and helped clean up from breakfast. When they were done, the girls nervously followed James into the family room to talk.

Ava rubbed her sore ass as she stared at Abbey, then sat down. Ava realized she liked the bite that was left behind from the spanking.

Hannah was the first to talk. "Does this mean we call you master now?"

"No, here at home, and if it is just us, you will call me James. If we are with others from the community, you will call me Sir or Ma'am."

"Can I ask why?" asked Sara.

"It is out of respect. I am a Dom/Domme in our community," he explained.

"So...I have a question, and you don't get to spank me for it," Ava said, lifting her chin.

"This is a neutral space; we are discussing the lifestyle and what happened this morning. As long as you are respectful, there is no fear of punishment," James said as he sat beside Ava.

"Careful, heifer, he sat that close last night when he grabbed me," Abbey warned.

"Yes, I was. But tell Ava what you did wrong."

"I disrespected him and didn't answer when asked to."

"Well, now that we have that out of the way. I want to talk to all of you about last night. Now that you all know who I truly am, what do you think?" James asked.

"I told you last night that I love who you are," said Abbey.

"I like who you are. I like that you are more confident and don't give a shit what people think," said Ava.

"I like who you are," Hannah chimed in.

"You scare the shit out of me. But I still like you," Sara said quietly.

"Does anyone have questions about last night?" asked James.

"I do," said Hannah. "Why did you flip out when we walked into the club?"

"Because four single women walked into a BDSM sex club not knowing anything about the lifestyle," James said calmly.

"To our defense, we did not know it was that kind of club," said Ava.

"Well, Abbey was told to forget about Fetish. I told her it was not a place for her," James shot back.

"I am glad I didn't listen, because I now know who you are, and the lifestyle calls to me," Abbey said proudly.

"I understand that, sis. You girls were in danger. You girls stood out like sore thumbs to predators. I will say this one more time so everyone will understand. In the BDSM world, men and women that claim they are Doms and Dommes will pray on people who know nothing. All they are out there to be controlling over new submissives. If you are interested in this lifestyle, I will help you as much as possible. I will also teach you how to find a respectful Dom, or Domme, whichever you choose."

"I am interested in learning," Ava said quietly.

"Me too," added Hannah.

James looked at Sara and thought she looked like a scared little mouse. "Sara, my new love, how are you feeling about all this?" James asked, trying to calm her down.

"This is all kinda scary. I know NOTHING about this side of life," Sara said as her face turned dark pink.

"Sara, there is no reason to be scared. This is just another side to having a sex life. Was there anything that called to you?" he asked.

Sara looked at her lap and shrugged her shoulders.

"Did I say something wrong?" he asked.

"No. She can't answer your questions. She does not know what a sex life is. Sara is a virgin," Hannah blurted out.

"Hannah, you're an ass! Why would you put her business out there for everyone?" Abbey snapped.

James was dumbfounded. He stood and paced as the anger rose. When he couldn't hold it in any longer, he exploded.

"YOU CRAZY BITCHES TOOK A VIRGIN TO A FUCK-ING SEX CLUB...A BDSM SEX CLUB, TO BE EXACT. WHAT THE FUCK WERE YOU THINKING. WHEN YOU SEEN WHAT FETISH WAS, YOU SHOULD HAVE FUCKING LEFT AS I ASKED YOU TOO!!!!" he screamed at the top of his lungs.

James noticed that his screaming had made Sara cry. He sat beside her and cradled her in his arms, murmuring.

"Shhh, baby girl. There is no reason for tears. I am so sorry I scared you by yelling. I am here to protect you, no matter what. I will even protect you from these bitches if needed. I am so sorry they forced you to witness what you did last night. I hope nothing you saw scared you."

No one dared to say anything. They sat quietly, watching how different James truly was. Sara had always been an ugly crier, but James had her quiet in minutes. The girls watched in awe as James sat her back down on the couch, keeping her tucked safely in his side.

"Sara, do you want to stay for the rest of this discussion, or would you like to leave?" he asked softly.

"I would like to stay. I have some questions. I liked some of the stuff I saw. It did not embarrass me because I am a virgin. It was because some of the stuff called to me, and I do not know why? Last night was the first night I had ever masturbated," she said, turning pink again.

James put a finger under Sara's chin and tipped up her face. When he looked into her pretty blue eyes, he leaned in and kissed her softly.

"As I am the first Dom talking to you, let me give you your first lesson. You are a beautiful woman. Let what happened last night empower you," James said, smiling.

Abbey's heart burst with love for her brother; she knew he had opened his heart to her friends. He loved them just like he loved her. She was pulled back to reality when she heard James talking.

"Sara, what questions do you have for me?" asked James.

"Why don't you have a submissive?" Sara asked.

"Oh, sweet baby girl. I have many. The ones I scened with last night are just two of my subs," he smiled, showing his teeth.

"Oh. If it is like that, I don't think I can live this lifestyle," Sara said quietly.

"It is not always like this. There are many Doms and Dommes that have only one submissive. I have many because I have not found that special one. When I do, trust and believe me, there will be a collar in their future," he said wistfully.

"So, Bubs. Will they be wearing a protection collar?" asked Abbey.

"Yes... There will be a list of rules you ladies will follow. Not only to respect me but to help you learn when you find a Dom or Domme.

1. You will wear the protection collar at all times.

2. You will not attend Fetish unaccompanied. You may only attend with me unless I have approved the Dom.

3. You will wear only the proper attire when you attend the club.

4. You will pay attention to your surroundings at all times.

5. You will NEVER put yourself in danger again.

6. When you are in the presence of our community, you will respect me by only calling me Sir or Ma'am.

7. You will not scene with any Dom unless I have vetted them. This is strictly for your safety.

8. The use of illegal drugs will not be tolerated.

9. If you drink, NEVER drink more than your limit.

"Do you all agree with these rules?" James asked.

The girls looked at each other, then at James, and said in unison, "Yes, Sir."

James nodded, then left the room. They talked while they waited for him to return.

"Hey, Abbey, thank you for sticking up for me," Sara said quietly.

"Hannah, what you did to Sara was a bitch move," Ava snapped.

"I am sorry, Sara. I just said something because I knew you were too scared to say anything," apologized Hannah.

When James returned, he held four black leather collars with tiny hearts that dangled in the front and a lock in the back. One by one, James placed the collars on the girls.

"Now, tonight, we will go to Fetish, and I will introduce you to the community. I know you ladies have a full day planned, so I will send my personal shopper to collect your outfits for tonight. Ava, you will tell your manager and photographer that the collar is non-negotiable. Sara, the salt water will not hurt your collar, so there is no need to worry about that. Hannah, your collar will be part of your suit for court. Abbey, that will be the same for you. My point is the collars stay on. You might as well get used to wearing them all the time now because if you find your Dom and he offers you a collar...that collar will be a part of you for the rest of your life. Now you all have a busy day ahead of you. Enjoy your day, ladies, and I will see you back here at seven sharp. That way, you have an hour and a half to make yourself club-ready. Welcome to my world," James said as he left the room and climbed the stairs to start his day.

Chapter 9

Abbey~

As the girls explored Dallas, Abbey thought about the number burning a hole in her pocket.

"Are you thinking about that damn number again?" asked Ava.

"Yes, I don't know if I should call or text him. Or should I wait and see him at the club tonight?" Abbey sighed.

"How do you know he will even be at the club? Just because his dad owns the place doesn't mean he will be there. Just text him and ask," challenged Ava.

Abbey sighed, pulled out her phone, and sat on a bench outside the Uptown Dallas Plaza. She unlocked her phone and typed in the number.

Abbey: Hello.

ZayShawn: Hello, Ms. Abbey.

Abbey: How did you know it was me?

ZayShawn: Well, sweetheart, you are the only person I have given my number to.

Abbey: Why do I find that hard to believe?

ZayShawn: I do not lie. Plus, I have given you no reason not to trust me.

Abbey: I don't trust easily.

ZayShawn: I will enjoy earning your trust, Baby Girl. So I take it you have more questions for me?

Abbey: Yes...Ummm...I have decided to see if the BDSM lifestyle is for me. James is taking us to the club tonight, and I wanted to know if you will be there.

ZayShawn: What did James say about you talking to me?

Abbey: Well...He gave me your number, didn't he?

ZayShawn: I would love to be the one who teaches you as long as I have James' blessing.

Abbey: I am a big girl...I can make my own decisions.

ZayShawn: First lesson...I will not touch you unless I have his blessing.

Abbey: I am not trying to be difficult. But why do you need his blessing?

ZayShawn: First, James Brewer is one of the most respected Doms in our community. Second, he is your family.

Abbey: I can respect that.

ZayShawn: We will pick up this conversation this evening. I need to go; the siren just started screaming. Until tonight, my blue-haired beauty.

Abbey stood, shoved her phone into her back pocket, and looked for her friends. She spotted them sitting outside a little bistro, eating lunch. She loved they gave her some space to contact ZayShawn. Abbey joined her friends and smiled when she noticed her friends had ordered her lunch and a sweet tea. They ate lunch and talked and wondered about what they would learn tonight.

~ZayShawn~

Visions of Abbey invaded ZayShawn's thoughts as he put on his fire-fighting gear. Even though he was the Fire Marshal, he never asked his men to run into a fire alone. As Abbey took the first bite of her lunch, ZayShawn ran into the burning highrise.

~Abbey~

After lunch, the girls reported to the companies they would work for. Hannah was accepted into a law firm where she could one day make partner. The girls went on a tour of her new job at the aquarium with Sara. Ava set up a time for her photo shoot with her new manager, and

Abbey signed her contract with her new realty company. Overall, they had a perfect day. Shortly after five, they headed home.

The girls came to a halt in the family room when they saw four women kneeling, hands lying on their laps, palms up, and heads bowed.

"Umm…Hello, who are you, and why are you in my brother's house?" Abbey asked.

"They will not answer you, little sister," James' voice rang out behind her.

The girls turned, and Abbey's mouth fell open at the sight of her brother. James was bare-chested with faded blue jeans that hung low on his hips, revealing a very built body. He was barefooted, with a white gold chain around his neck with four different colored keys. While he studied his new wards, he swirled his old-fashioned glass of peanut butter whiskey on the rocks.

"Why won't they answer her?" asked Sara nervously.

"Because I have instructed them to kneel and wait for my next command," James said as he sipped.

"Oh…" Abbey said softly.

"Well, I guess we will leave you to it then," Ava said, trying to sneak off.

"Stop, please…I need to talk to you guys," James said as he smiled, putting the girls at ease. "Please come in here and have a seat."

"Are we in trouble?" Abbey asked as they sat on the couch.

"Not at all. I have a gift for each of you," he said, walking into the room.

"I like gifts," Abbey smiled.

"I said I would help you in any way I could. These four ladies are my best submissives. They are your new bosom buddies. They will help your transition into the lifestyle a little easier. Then, after you all decide that this lifestyle is for you, we will talk to Mistress Raven about training you properly. So until then, ladies, I would love to introduce you to Lily, Rose, Dahlia, and Orchid. Rise, my lovely Pets, and meet my baby sisters."

Abbey watched as the submissives stood gracefully. She noticed each one had a necklace with a flower that matched their names.

"Be free, my Pets. You may now relax and socialize. Also, let me introduce you to Abbey, Ava, Hannah, and Sarah. Rose, you will help Abbey. Orchid, you will help Ava. Dahlia, you will help Sara and Lily; you will help Hannah. My Pets will help you dress and ready yourself to attend Fetish. They will teach you what is proper attire and what is taboo in the club. Have fun, my darlings. This will be a big night for you," James said as he finished his whiskey.

"I have a couple of questions if it is okay, Sir," Abbey said.

"Questions are always welcome, sis. We are in our home, and you are not my submissive. When we are at home, you can call me James," he said, opening his arms to her.

Without hesitation, Abbey went into her brother's welcoming embrace. James held her tight and whispered, "See, I told you that you would not lose me as your brother. I will always be your brother first. I love you, Abbs," he said, kissing the top of her head.

Abbey reached up, fingered the keys on the chain around his neck, and asked, "What are these for?"

"These keys go to your collars. Blue is yours, red is Ava's, yellow is Hannah's, and purple is Sara's," he explained.

"Oh...cool. Umm...I texted ZayShawn today," she said quietly.

Abbey felt James' body quiver when she said ZayShawn's name.

Before continuing his conversation with Abbey, he looked at the others and said, "I need to talk to Abbey. The rest of you can go get ready for the club."

They watched the other chatter and walked away, leaving Rose behind.

"Rose, you are more than welcome to stay here, or you can wait for me in my room," Abbey said sweetly.

"I would like to wait for you, Miss Abbey," Rose said, smiling.

"Rose, there is no reason for you to call me Miss. Just call me Abbey."

"Oh, no, Ma'am...I can't do that. You are Sir's sister. Calling you anything other than Miss Abbey would be disrespectful," stammered Rose.

"Rose, I am also being trained to be a submissive. So calling me Abbey is not disrespectful," Abbey said, smiling.

"Rose, my beautiful Pet. I want you to mentor her. So her transition into her new lifestyle is easier. I know you both will become friends."

Rose nodded and sat on the floor at James' feet. He sat on the couch and softly placed his hand on the top of her head. Abbey smiled as she watched the interaction between James and his sub. When she laid her head on his lap, he turned his head and said, "What have you decided?"

"I told him I wanted to see if the lifestyle was for me, and he said we could talk tonight at the club. He also said he would not touch me unless he had your blessing," Abbey explained.

"That makes me want to punch his face a little less," he grumbled.

"Why would you say that? You said you liked him. That he can be trusted?" asked Abbey.

"You are my sister. Can you date anyone you choose? Yes! Can you live any lifestyle you desire? Yes! That doesn't mean I like it. Do I want to think about someone whipping and fucking the shit out of the one person my world spins for? No. But you are grown and live the way you want to live. I vow to be here for you in any way you need. Now, if that son of a bitch hurts you, I will kill him. With that being said, I will give my blessing. I will tell him the same when I see him tonight," James said, feeling defeated.

Abbey kissed James on the cheek before standing, holding her hand to Rose. Rose looked up at James, and when he nodded his head, she smiled and placed her hand into Abbey's.

After Abbey and Rose were upstairs to where prying ears were far enough away, he grumbled while pulling out his phone., "What the fuck have I done...I have opened up a halfway house for subs in training. I need to call LaMarkus and Faye."

The girls felt empowered in their new attire for the club. He had them dressed in corsets that boosted their breast, making them fetching to the eyes. They were in black micro skirts with black hoes with a dark seam running up the back of the legs. They were wearing matching black Prada pumps. James had the corset color match the keys around his neck.

James wore a black polo unbuttoned showing his tanned chest. He was still wearing the low-riding faded jeans with black Wingtip Oxfords. Everyone's heads turned when he entered the club with the girls in tow. It wasn't very often James attended the club as himself. But it didn't matter if he showed up as James or Chuckalisa. He always had respect.

Part 2

Submission

A truly submissive woman is to be treasured, cherished and protected for it is only she who can give a man the gift of dominance.

~ Anne Desclos

Chapter 10

James walked up to the bar where Faye and LaMarkus were seated, "Good Evening, LaMarkus...Good Evening Faye, you're looking as beautiful as ever. I want to introduce you to my girls. This is Abbey, Ava, Sara, and Hannah. They are new to Dallas and new to the lifestyle. Faye darling, would you please keep an eye on them while I have a much-needed conversation with your son?" James asked sweetly.

"James, can we have a few words before you doom my son? I have a bad feeling you are about to threaten to toss him in the bowels of hell," asked LaMarkus.

"I think that would be wise. I have a lot of respect for you and Faye, and I wouldn't want this to change anything," James answered.

Abbey watched James and LaMarkus disappear to some seating behind a curtain and thought, *OH SHIT!!!*

"Well, hello. You all look very exquisite," Faye said, enticing them to engage in conversation.

"Why, thank you, Miss Faye," Sara said, blushing.

"So, where are you ladies from?" she asked.

"We are from a tiny town," Hannah said.

"Middlesboro, Kentucky," answered Abbey.

Ava watched the elegant sub. She had long black wavy hair and beautiful light blue eyes, wearing a black and purple corset with spider web lace. Her leather pants had zippers from hip to foot for easy removal and simple black pumps. Her collar was black leather with a jeweled spider that dangled in front.

Faye locked eyes with Ava and smiled. "Are you always quiet, or are you trying to see if I am a danger to you and your sisters?" she asked.

"A little of both. This world is very enticing. We have been warned to keep an eye on our surroundings. So before I open up and let anyone in, I will ensure we are safe," Ava tested.

"Smart girl. Well, I am someone you can trust. I know it will take you time to realize that. If you have questions, you girls can always come to me," she said, handing them a card with her number.

Abbey got uneasy when she noticed Ava was on the defensive. She had always thought Ava was like a viper, silent but deadly when she struck. If Ava ever thought any of the people she loved were in danger, they better call the armed forces to contain her. When James returned with LaMarkus, the worry eased until he said, "Abbey, please join me and ZayShawn."

"Yes, Sir," answered Abbey.

She followed James back to the same seating area where he had just come from. When she passed through the curtain, Abbey noticed ZayShawn was already seated, sipping on his crown apple on the rocks. ZayShawn sat his glass down and stood, taking Abbey's hand in his and placed a soft kiss on her knuckles.

"Good evening, my blue-haired beauty."

"Good evening..."

"For now, you may call me ZayShawn."

"Good evening, ZayShawn."

"Abbey, please have a seat," James commanded.

Abbey took the seat next to James and waited quietly to find out what was going to happen next.

"ZayShawn...Abbey told me she contacted you earlier in the day. She also informed me you told her you would not touch her without my blessing. First, let me say thank you for the respect you have shown me by asking for my blessing. Second, thank you for having enough respect for her and letting her decide to call you. Now, I will talk to you as her brother. Abbey is the most important person in my life. She is smart, beautiful, caring, loving, strong-willed, and the most trustworthy person I have ever met. She may choose who she wants to be with and how to live her life, even if it makes me itchy. I know she can take care of herself, but I reserve the right to whoop your ass if you hurt her. Now, with that being said, I give you both my blessing," James said as he kissed Abbey on the cheek and left.

ZayShawn patted the spot next to him on the couch. "Come sit here."

Abbey nervously slid over to the spot closer to ZayShawn. Once she was next to him, she could smell his cologne. It was intoxicating to her senses. She looked up into his sexy brown eyes and felt a spark. Now that they had her brother's blessing, she was excited and scared as hell, all at the same time. "Yes, ZayShawn," she said.

"I want to let you know, my blue-haired beauty, that anything that happens from here out is entirely up to you and your comfort level. Yes, we will push the boundaries, but if you truly do not like anything that we decide to try, you have the right to stop me without any consequences. Do you understand?" asked ZayShawn.

Abbey tried to look confident and asked, "No consequences at all?"

"None at all."

"Ok."

"Now, do you have any questions?"

"Well, I have done a little research online about it, and I know that every Dom has certain props that they prefer. What are yours?" she asked him.

"Personally, I prefer the bullwhip, and the paddle. Really any impact play items, if that's what you're asking. But as far as other things, I would like to see what you like or are interested in, and we can work up from there. What else did you learn while consulting Google?"

"Well, I saw some things that were interesting and pretty straightforward. But there was some terrifying stuff on there, too."

"First, you know Google is not your friend, right?" he said with a smile.

Abbey shyly smiled and dropped her eyes to her lap in embarrassment.

ZayShawn lifted her chin and said, "Don't be embarrassed. You went to the only place you knew of at the time to try to learn, and that means a lot. So, first, tell me what was interesting to you."

Abbey smiled innocently and said. "Well, bondage and impact play really got me. But then I saw those things that look like clothes pins that were put on your nipples, and I was like, 'Whoa, that looks nice.' Let's see...Oh, that thing where you tie someone up and suspend her in the air...that looks sexy."

"Knowing that bondage and impact play are things you may like makes me very happy. Those 'clothespins' are called nipple clamps. There are also genital clamps as well. And it sounds like you were talking about kinbaku. If this relationship works out and leads somewhere promising, I will take classes on the subject to keep you happy. I only want to see a smile on your face at all times." ZayShawn said with a sincere look on his face.

All Abbey could do at that moment was smile. This man just said all the right things to make her melt in the seat.

"Now, what are some of the things that scared you?"

"Well, that fire thing that Chuckalisa did the other night is one of them, the men wearing masks. I didn't find much online, so I will admit that I have a lot to learn. Then there were those weird-looking dildo things that were really short and kinda egg-shaped with a stopper on the end of it. I have no damn idea what those were or what they were for."

ZayShawn let out a quiet laugh at her description. "First, the fire does not hurt or burn. It is called Fireplay. The fire doesn't last long enough to do any damage. Masks are strictly a preference that some Doms have. I, personally, do not like them. When I require my sub to look at me, I want her to see my face and expressions." ZayShawn couldn't hold back the chuckle any longer when he said, "And the 'weird egg-shaped dildo' is called a butt plug. I think the name speaks for itself."

Abbey's eyes widened as what ZayShawn said sunk in, "Oh no, no, no! Those don't go in there, do they?!"

"Yes, they do."

"Nope! Not happening! Don't toucha the butt!!"

ZayShawn smiled and said. "I can see that is a hard limit for you. How about we agree to at least try to have a discussion about it later and see if you still feel that way? Remember, we will test those boundaries."

Abbey looked at ZayShawn and felt strongly that he wouldn't do anything to hurt or scare her, so she nodded in agreement.

"Good. Now, is there anything else that you want to know about me or the lifestyle?"

"Well, I also read on Google that a lot of Doms have multiple subs and dabble in a somewhat swinger lifestyle. Do you?"

"Honestly, no. I am not only looking for a sub; I am looking for THE ONE. I want a relationship like my dad and Faye have. I want a marriage like any other person and a family...one day."

"Good. Because I am not into multiples or sharing." She smiled as she looked into his eyes. There was something about his eyes that made her feel so relaxed.

"Good. Neither am I. Would you like to make our entrance now?" asked ZayShawn.

Abbey nodded as he stood and took her hand. They walked out into the club hand in hand, both of them smiling. ZayShawn let go of her hand and placed his hand on the small of her back to lead her over to where his family was sitting, along with her family.

As Abbey looked around the club, she noticed everyone was looking their way. ZayShawn felt her tense up as her nerves began to take over. He reached his hand around to her waist and gave it a slight squeeze so that she looked up into his eyes and immediately calmed.

I can't believe this man has this effect on me already.

As they approached the table where their families were seated, James stood up and shook ZayShawn's hand before hugging his little sister. Both James and ZayShawn nodded, and ZayShawn motioned for Abbey to have a seat before he took his place next to her.

As the night progressed, they talked and watched various people scene throughout the club. Abbey tapped ZayShawn and whispered in his ear, "When do you think we could try a scene?"

"Well, I am glad you asked. We are up next," he said with a shit-eating grin on his face.

"Wait...What?"

ZayShawn stood and held his hand out for Abbey to take. She placed her shaky hand in his when she stood. James shifted uneasily in his seat as he watched his baby sister walk the last few steps as an innocent in the BDSM world. Abbey shook with anticipation and fear when they were on stage as she waited for his first command while she watched him step into his Dom role.

"When we are in the community, you will call me Sir. When we are scening, you will call me Daddy. Do you understand, Beauty?"

"Yes," she said quietly.

"Yes, what, Beauty?"

"Yes, Daddy."

"Good girl," he purred.

The feeling she felt when he called her a good girl made the fear disappear. Abbey now knew she desperately wanted to please him.

"We will start slow and work our way up from there. Normally, I would not tell you what we would be doing. But considering this is your first time, I will tell you step by step. If we do anything you do not agree with, or if it brings you non-pleasurable pain, you are to use a safe word. We haven't covered safe words yet, so you will only use Green, Yellow, and Red tonight. Green is you are good. Yellow is you are at your limit, and Red means stop. Understand?"

"Yes, Daddy," she said more confidently.

"Tonight will be light and easy. First, I will bind you with my leather cuffs and place you on my St. Andrew's Cross. Then I will undress you from the waist up. Then I will let you feel the kiss of my whip. If you are a good girl, I will even let you cum. How does that sound, Beauty?"

"It sounds yummy, Daddy," she said with excitement in her eyes.

ZayShawn left her standing in the center of the stage and went to the wall of cuffs. He had chosen black leather cuffs with red roses painted on them. When he was standing in front of Abbey, he said, "Look at the cuffs, Beauty."

"Oh, they are pretty," she said, holding her wrists out to him.

"Do you like them?"

"Yes, they are gorgeous."

"Then I will tell you what. After tonight, if you feel the lifestyle is for you, I will have some crafted for you for our playroom."

Abbey smiled shyly and nodded.

ZayShawn quickly bound Abbey's hands in the soft leather cuffs and led her to the St. Andrew's Cross. He lifted each arm and clipped each cuff to the rings. Then he braided her long blue hair and tied it into a loose knot. Before she started unlacing her corset, he placed a soft kiss on the crook of her neck. When the top half of her was finally bare, ZayShawn ran his hand across her soft skin.

ZayShawn leaned over and whispered, "Beauty, you are just as I had dreamed last night. You are a goddess."

Abbey blushed with her whole body, turning her exposed skin a light pink. Before he walked over to collect his bullwhip, he smacked her ass, making it jiggle. Abbey moaned when his hand connected with her ass making him grin.

"Beauty, I will snap my whip next to you so you can get familiar with her sound. I also need you to stay still. If you move, my aim will be off, and I can accidentally hurt you. Do you understand, Beauty?"

"Yes, Daddy."

"Good girl," he purred.

ZayShawn cracked the whip a few times on each side until she relaxed. Before connecting, he said, "I will give you six soft kisses."

The next snap of the whip kissed the back of Abbey's left shoulder, then the right. ZayShawn moved back and forth between her shoulders, warming up her skin to complete the first set of strikes.

After the sixth strike, he asked, "Color, Beauty?"

"Green, Daddy," she said with excitement.

"Good, now I am going to add some music. This time, the kisses will be a little harder. I will keep increasing the strikes until we meet your limit. I want you to call out Yellow as soon as we get there. Understand?"

"Yes, Daddy."

ZayShawn pushed play on the mp3 player, and Bach rang through the speakers. Then he went to the wall and picked up a leg holster and a toy from his bag. He knelt to fasten the holster on her leg and talked to her softly, "You have done very well, Beauty, and I like to reward good girls. This will help you relax while you receive the next set of lashes."

After placing the toy in the holster, she realized the toy pressed against her pussy, targeting the clit.

"Daddy?"

"Yes, Beauty," he answered.

"What is that?"

"That is called a Hitachi Wand," he said, smiling.

"What does it do?"

"That I will let you find out."

ZayShawn cracked the whip beside her to let her know he was ready. With each strike, the kiss of the whip bit harder. When the kiss of the whip left pink lines, Abbey said, "Yellow."

"Okay, Beauty. My whip will kiss your skin just like this six times. But I will reward you since you have been such a good girl."

ZayShawn pulled a remote from his pocket and turned on the Hitachi Wand.

"Holy Crap!!" Abbey cried out, making ZayShawn chuckle.

When she was still, he said, "As my whip kisses your skin, focus on the wand. When I tell you too, I want you to cum for me. Can you do that, Beauty?"

"I don't know, but I want to try," she said, unsure.

With each kiss of the whip, he turned the wand on a higher setting. When the third kiss landed, Abbey moaned. ZayShawn could tell Abbey was close to subspace when her moan increased with each kiss. When he delivered the last kiss, he growled, "Come for Daddy!"

Abbey's body responded to ZayShawn's voice, and she screamed when she came. Her body shook from the powerful orgasm, leaving her spent and sagging on the cross. ZayShawn nodded at the bouncer to close the curtain and unhooked Abbey from the cross.

Chapter 11

When Abbey woke, she found herself lying on ZayShawn's chest, and he was softly stroking her back.

"Welcome back, Beauty," ZayShawn purred.

"Mmmm...this is nice," Abbey said with a yawn.

"Did you enjoy tonight?"

"Yes, Daddy, I did."

"What did you think about the Hitachi Wand?"

"That damn thing is the devil," she said, causing him to chuckle.

"But did you like it?"

"Yes."

When his hand stopped moving, she tried to snuggle in. When ZayShawn slapped her ass, Abbey yelped.

"What did you do that for?"

"What did you forget? How do you answer me?"

"Yes, Daddy?"

"That is correct. Even though it is aftercare, this is still considered part of the scene."

"I'm sorry, Daddy. It won't happen again."

"Good girl. Now we need to clean up our mess. That way, it is clean for the next couple," he said.

When everything was clean, ZayShawn helped her lace her corset and fix her hair. When they rejoined the others, Abbey noticed Sara had a sour look that could kill someone ten times over.

"Sara, what is wrong?" Abbey asked.

"She's not allowed to talk. She's on punishment," Hannah explained.

"What the hell did she do?" Abbey asked.

"She was disrespectful," Ava answered.

Abbey leaned over to James and asked, "Who was she disrespectful to, Sir?"

"Abbey now is not the time to talk about it," James said sternly.

"Yes, Sir," Abbey answered quietly and sipped her drink ZayShawn had ordered.

"Abbey, I would like to introduce you to my family," said ZayShawn.

"Even though you have already met her, this remarkable woman helped raise me and my brothers, Faye. She is my father's girlfriend, submissive, and part owner of this club. The handsome man next to her is my father, LaMarkus. You may call him Mr. LaMarkus. The good-looking devil next to my father is my oldest brother, Terrance. You may call him Mr. Terry. The goofy looking one next to the eldest is my older brother Xavier. You may call him Mr. X. Last, my boy, Brad, is the white boy sitting next to your friend. You may call him Mr. Jones. Everyone, this is Abbey."

"It is nice to meet you all. Sir, I would like to introduce you to my friends. You know my brother, sitting next to Mr. Terry, is Sara. Hannah is sitting next to Mr. Jones. That leaves Ava, who is sitting next to Mr. X."

"It is nice to meet you, lovely ladies. You may call me Master Shawn. If I may ask, how was your first night in our world?"

"I have thoroughly enjoyed myself. I can see myself living this lifestyle," Ava said with bright eyes.

"I have already decided after our scene that the lifestyle is a yes for me." Abbey blushed.

"I was all in last night when we crashed into the club," Hannah said, smiling.

When ZayShawn looked at Sara, she sat there quietly. After about five seconds, Sara looked at Terrance and said, "I am sorry for being a disrespectful brat and trying to show off to my friends. It won't happen again, Mr. Terry."

"I accept your apology, and if you are ready to be a good girl, you may join your friends in the conversation," Terrance said, as he kissed her knuckles.

Sara nodded and looked over at ZayShawn. "I like the lifestyle, but I have a lot to learn. I guess with time, I will answer your question confidently."

"If I may suggest, you ladies should take a few courses from Mistress Ravan. She will handle any questions you have. Plus, you will learn what we will expect of you as a submissive," Faye offered.

As the night wound down, James noticed the girls were getting tired. So he stood and said, "Well, my friends, it has been fun. My girls are getting tired, and they all start their jobs in the morning. I bid you all good night."

The girls stood and said their goodnights. Ava, Hannah, and Sara walked with James to his SUV. Abbey and ZayShawn walked behind the group with his hand on her lower back. When they reached the SUV, ZayShawn spun Abbey to where her back was pressed against the truck; lifting her arms, he gripped her wrist in one hand, then crushed his mouth to hers. Abbey opened and submitted to him instantly. When ZayShawn broke the kiss, Abbey wanted to slide bonelessly to the ground and crave more. He snuck one arm around her and pulled her to him while he used the other hand to open the door. He kissed her softly one last time and said good night. When Abbey was safely in the SUV, ZayShawn pushed the door closed and walked past the entrance to the club, disappearing into the dark parking lot.

It surprised James when the car ride was quiet on the way home; he figured there would be all kinds of girl chatter all the way home. When he looked in the rear-view mirror, he saw Sara staring out the window with silent tears running down her cheeks. Ava was whispering with Hannah, and when he looked at the front seat passenger, he saw Abbey was fast asleep with a smile.

When they pulled into the driveway, Abbey opened her eyes. When the girls exited the SUV, he said, "Ava, Hannah, can you please ensure Abbey gets up the stairs unharmed? I want to talk to Sara."

"Yep…We got her," Ava and Hannah chimed.

"Sara, can you please come with me?" asked James.

Sara nodded quietly, followed James into the living room, and sat down. When he looked at her beautiful face, she still had tear-stained cheeks.

"Why all the tears, little dove?" James asked.

"Because I am so confused," she said quietly.

"Tell me about it, and maybe I can help."

"I understand why I got punished...but why did you let him punish me?"

"In this world, you must remember the rules. You disrespected Terrance; therefore, he had the right to punish you. Did he hurt you?"

"No."

"Then I don't understand...why were you crying?"

"Because it excited me. When Mr. Terry manhandled me and then spanked me...It made me wet. I'm not used to anything making me wet. I am a virgin, for Christ's sake."

"Little Dove, in this lifestyle, you will learn all sorts of different things about your body. Don't let them hold you back or scare you. Let the information you learn empower you. Don't let your mouth overload your sexy little ass in the wrong setting anymore. So was it the punishment or the man that made you wet?"

"That is another thing that is confusing me. I don't know. I want to say it was the punishment, but I am afraid it was the man. In every way, he is not my type. He makes me mad. Some of the things he said to me tonight...I just wanted to punch him in the face. Sara, the scared little mouse, was called a brat, and I was showing off to my friends. I have never shown off a day in my life. He doesn't even fucking know me," Sara said as she stood and started stomping around the room.

James sat back and smiled as he watched the girl he had known his whole life as quiet and shy throw a tantrum in his living room.

"Sara, my dove...Do you see what you are doing? You have crawled out of your shell and blossomed into a new woman. I witnessed everything you did tonight. You were acting bratty, and you were disrespectful. You flipped him the bird, and when you were talking to him, you called him Terrance five times after he told you to call him Mr. Terry. Therefore, you deserved to be punished."

Sara stopped her tirade and covered her face; she knew James was telling the truth. "Oh, my lord...I am such a spoiled brat," she whined.

"Now that you are aware, you can fix the problem. Now, we can talk more about this tomorrow. It would be best if you get some sleep; you start your new job in about six hours," James said sweetly, closing the conversation.

"But I wanna..."

"I said, good night, Sara. We will talk more tomorrow," James said sternly.

Sara decided it was best to shut her mouth and head to bed; she did not want to repeat what happened earlier tonight. As she got ready for bed, Sara thought about the events that had occurred earlier in the night.

Chapter 12

The following morning, Abbey stretched, and she could still feel the last few kisses from ZayShawn's whip. Abbey hoped that one day she could say the kisses came from her Daddy's whip. The feelings that were building in Abbey for ZayShawn scared the shit out of her.

Excited about her new job, she jumped out of bed and ran into the en-suite to shower. She was so wrapped up in getting ready for work she never saw the display on her phone light up from an incoming message.

After Abbey was dressed and ready for her first day, she snatched her phone from the bedside table and headed downstairs to find the others and get something to eat. She was greeted the same as the morning before; she found everyone at the breakfast bar. This morning James had prepared an everything bagel with cream cheese and a side of bacon. As Abbey ate breakfast, she checked her phone and smiled.

ZayShawn: Good Morning, Abbey. I hope you slept well and your first day is terrific. Dinner tonight to celebrate your first day.

Beauty...I am requesting for you to be ready by seven pm. Make sure you wear something black and semi-formal. NO PANTIES.

Until then, my Good Girl!

Sir

"Oh...I am super excited! ZayShawn texted me, but I am confused," Abbey said, holding her phone out to James.

James looked at the phone, smiled, and said, "This means ZayShawn wants to take you to dinner to celebrate your new job. But at some point tonight, you will step into your D/S roles."

Abbey smiled and ate the rest of her breakfast, daydreaming about tonight's festivities. James picked up her plate and placed it in the dishwasher when she had finished eating.

"Bubs... I'm not complaining, but why do you make us breakfast every morning?"

"Well, I wasn't. I was going to let you hoes fend for yourselves...but that has changed. Now that I am protecting four new subs, my duty and pleasure as a Dom is to care for my submissives."

"Well, I can speak for all of us when I say...we love it," she said as she kissed James. Abbey turned and ran out of the house. When James heard the front door open again, he laughed. He laughed harder when he saw Abbey's face, making his stomach hurt and a tear slide down his cheek.

"What's so damn funny, brother?"

"Let me ask you this, sister of mine. How are you getting to work?" he asked with a wide smile resembling the Cheshire cat.

"I guess I will be calling for an Uber if you don't take me."

"I guess you can take one of mine," he laughed and jingled keys.

"James Charles Brewer...You, sir, are a dick," she said, fisting her hands on her hips.

"Hey now...I'm just having a little fun. No reason to be salty."

Abbey flipped him the bird and stomped off to the garage.

"Whoo. She's lucky that she did that here and not the club, or she would have been going to work with a sore ass," Sara said, taking a sip of her coffee, trying to hide her smile.

By noon, Abbey had shown three houses and still had two open houses to go to after lunch. Abbey ate lunch with a couple of colleagues and went straight to her first open house of the afternoon. After the open house, she returned to the office, excited to announce she had three offers for the last place she just showed. When she entered her office, she saw a beautiful potted black lily with a red ribbon and a card. She opened the card and read.

Welcome to the community, Ms. Abbey. I very much enjoyed your first scene last night. ZayShawn and James told me you are new to the lifestyle. If you ever have questions or would like to take some lessons, please feel free to contact me. I am excited to meet you.

Mistress Ravan

Abbey didn't know how to feel receiving gifts from strangers, but she remembered James, ZayShawn, and Faye saying she could trust her. Abbey decided to worry about it later, so she put the card in her purse and gathered the notes she needed for the last open house of the day. Abbey was excited that her last open house went great, but she was ecstatic that the day was finally over and she could get ready for her date with ZayShawn. She turned up the music and zoomed towards home. When red and blue flashing bubble gum lights flashed in her rearview mirror, she looked down at her speed and said, "Well fuck." she quickly pulled over and waited for the officer to approach the driver's window. All hope she could talk herself out of getting a ticket went out the window when Officer Brad Jones said, "Good afternoon, Ms. Abbey. Can I have your license and registration?"

"Yes, One second please...Umm...I don't want to get in any more trouble than I am. So what do I call you?"

"When I am at work, you can call me Officer Jones," he chuckled.

"Okay...Thank you, Officer Jones."

After Abbey handed Brad her license and James' registration, she sat quietly, hoping he would go easy on her.

"Why were you driving so fast, Abbey?"

"Well...Today was my first day at my new job, and I am excited that ZayShawn is picking me up for dinner at seven. I was in a fantastic mood, and I let it and the music get to my head. I am really sorry. It won't happen again."

"I will let you off with a warning this time. Just promise me you will take the lead out of your foot," he said, handing back her paperwork.

Brad tipped his hat to Abbey and walked back to his cruiser. Abbey pulled back into traffic and drove the speed limit home.

When Abbey made it home, she took off her pumps and ran through the house, and when she was just about to hit the stairs, she heard....

"Abigale Brown...Why the fuck did Brad just call me, telling me you were putting yourself in danger?" yelled James.

"Later, James...We will talk about it later," she yelled back.

"The fuck we will. We will talk about this NOW!" he growled.

"Fine...But you will have to come up here. I am running behind," she sighed.

Abbey started stripping when she entered her room to prepare for her date.

"Well, you wouldn't be running late if you didn't get pulled over because you were speeding," he said, leaning on her doorjamb.

"I know...I'm sorry I was speeding in your car. It won't happen again," she said, rolling her eyes.

"It being my car is not the fucking problem. What must I do to make it sink in that you can't put yourself in danger? Abbey, you are a submissive now. If you want this to work, you need to change the way you think. In this lifestyle, every action will have a reaction. For instance, if ZayShawn had gotten wind of this, you would not be spending the night celebrating. You would spend tonight dealing with your punishment. I told Brad I would take care of this, and there was no reason to call ZayShawn. But I expect you to tell him on your own. You have until the end of the night to tell him. If you don't, I will."

"Why did he call and tell you anyway?" Abbey snarled.

"Because we are a community, we look out for each other."

"Okay...I'm sorry. It won't happen again. I was feeling fantastic, and I got lost in the music. I promise."

"Okay. The box on the bed was delivered today," he said, walking over to her. "Please, Abbey, if you truly want to live in this lifestyle, you need to follow the rules," he said, kissing her forehead.

Just as James exited her room, she said, "I will work harder."

James nodded and left to get ready because his night was starting. Abbey went to the bed and pulled the string to untie the enormous red bow wrapped around the box. After lifting off the lid, she found a note.

Beauty,

I didn't know if you had anything to wear tonight, so I sent this over for you. I had James give me your size, so everything should fit. I am looking forward to seeing you tonight.

See you then,

Sir

Abbey placed the note card beside the box and opened the tissue paper. She found a lace stocking belt, silk stockings, a black strapless half-cup Demi bra, and a black cocktail dress inside the box. She unhooked her bra, letting it hit the floor. After she had put the new bra on, she realized it fit better than her old one. Next, she stepped into the lace stocking belt; turning, she sat down, sliding on the silk stocking and locking the grips onto the top, holding them in place. Abbey stood and pulled the dress out of the box. She unzipped the side, stepped into the dress, and pulled it up. After she zipped up the dress, she turned and looked in the mirror.

The dress was strapless, made from exceedingly soft cotton, and came to about mid-thigh. The silk stockings made her feel sexy, and the lace stocking belt with no panties made her feel naughty. She piled her curls on top of her head, letting a couple of tendrils hang. When she touched up her make-up, she changed her eye shadow to a gray and black smokey eye. As she finished the final touches, Chuckalisa knocked on her door; she was wearing a simple purple dress with black pumps. She wore a blond wig with tight spiral curls that hit about mid back. It pulled the whole outfit together between the makeup, necklace, and earrings.

"I figured you needed some ice to top that dress off," she said, holding out a necklace outfitted with black diamonds and earrings to match.

"Oh...they are stunning. Are you sure you want me to wear them?" Abbey asked.

"Yes. I want them back in the morning. Have fun tonight. Remember to ask him questions and get to know him. I mean him as ZayShawn and him as a Dom. Are you on birth control?" she asked.

"Yes, I am, and I will," Abbey said as she placed the back on the earrings she had just put on.

"Turn, darling, let me hook the necklace for you," Chuckalisa said, slipping it into place. "One more piece of advice. I don't know if you will end up at the club tonight. Considering what you are wearing, I don't think so. Remember when you are playing and if he does something that you don't like or it hurts...Use your safe word. If you don't have one, you can always use Red. If you need to use it, make sure it is loud enough that he can hear it. Plus, if you need me, I am only a phone call away. Have fun and try not to worry. I am taking the girls with me tonight," Chuckalisa said, cupping her cheeks.

"I will be careful, and I will remember my safe word if needed. Have fun and don't worry. If I need you, I will call. Now get out of here. You're late."

Chuckalisa looked at her watch and yelled, "Let's go, ladies. We are late."

Shortly after Chuckalisa and the girls left, she heard a car pull into the drive. She met him at the door. He was holding a dozen red roses and looked yummy. ZayShawn was wearing a black Gucci pinstripe suit and shiny black oxfords. He had his dreads pulled back in a low tail.

"Oh...Abbey, you are a vision," he said, handing her the roses and kissing her cheek.

"Thank you ZayShawn; you look very handsome as well. Let me put these in some water, and we can go," Abbey said, smiling.

Chapter 13

Abbey stared in awe at the car outside, waiting to take her on tonight's adventures.

"Is this beautiful beast yours?" she asked.

"Yes, it is," he said proudly.

"What is it?" she asked, walking around the car.

"It is a McLaren 720s. I bought it when I got promoted to Fire Marshal. Do you like it?"

"I love it," she sighed.

"Here, let me show off just a little," he said, grinning.

ZayShawn pulled a key fob from his pocket and pressed a button. The running lights under the black McLaren glowed blue.

"Very cool. Did you always have blue lights under the car?" she asked.

"Believe it or not...yes. Blue is my favorite color."

"Well, I like it."

ZayShawn smiled and opened the car door for Abbey. When she was safely tucked in, he shut the door. After ZayShawn climbed in behind the wheel, he looked at Abbey and asked, "Are you ready?"

Abbey nodded and smiled when the car had a low blue glow when the car started. As ZayShawn drove through the city, she listened to the radio. He had Keith Sweat playing just loud enough you don't need to strain to hear.

"What do you think of our town so far?" he asked.

"It is so different from where we grew up. Our town was so small. The Walmart and Post Office are the most significant things in our town. Dallas is so big and pretty at night when it comes alive. So when James called me and asked us to come down here, I jumped at the invitation. Plus, I missed my brother," she said, looking out the window.

"How are you and James related? If I may ask."

"James and I are childhood friends. I was the only one that was truly there for him growing up. The night he told his parents he was bi-sexual, his father kicked him out of the house. He stayed with me until he graduated high school that May. Then he left...I will never forget how lost I felt when he left. That's how I became so close with the girls. After James left, they swooped in and pulled me back out of my shell. We graduated and went to college; the day after graduation, we came here," Abbey explained.

Before ZayShawn could ask any more questions, they pulled up to the valet at one of the best five-star restaurants, Del Frisco. Abbey felt like a princess when her door was opened for her, and ZayShawn held out his hand to help her out of the car. He placed his hand on her lower back as they walked into the building.

He led her to the elevator and, pressing the button, said, "Tonight, my dear, you will dine with the city's best view."

When the doors opened, he led them over to the Maitre D.

"Reservation name, please," asked the Maitre D.

"Williams."

"Yes, Sir. William's party of two. Right this way," he said before scurrying off.

Their table was next to the wall of windows; they were on the restaurant's top floor. Abbey could see all the beautiful night lights of Dallas. ZayShawn pulled out her chair and waited for her to sit before seating himself on the other side. When the waiter showed up with the wine menu, he asked, "What would you like to eat tonight? Chicken, fish, or steak?"

"Oh...I don't know yet. I haven't seen the menu. I think I will have steak." replied Abbey.

ZayShawn nodded and looked at the wine menu.

"We will take Lafite Rothschild 1981," he said, closing the menu.

"At once, Sir," the waiter said, nodding.

Just as they were putting down the menus, the waiter returned with the bottle of wine. As the waiter poured the wine, ZayShawn said, "Leave the bottle."

"Yes, Sir. Have you decided on your meal?" he asked.

ZayShawn nodded at Abbey. "I would like the Charred Focaccia and steak salad with strawberry black pepper vinaigrette. I want my steak well done."

"For you, Sir?"

"I will have the Hanger Steak with Kimchi glaze and Miso Butter-grilled vegetables, with my steak cooked medium."

"Yes, Sir, your dinner will be here shortly," he said before disappearing into the kitchen.

While waiting for their dinner, Abbey and ZayShawn talked.

"How was your first day on the job?" he asked.

"My first day was good. I had three offers from my first open house. Then some other stuff happened, and now I am here."

"What kind of stuff?" he asked with a raised eyebrow.

"Well, I got a welcome gift, and I got pulled over on the way home."

"What kind of gift...And wait, what? You got pulled over?"

"I got a potted plant from Mistress Ravan with a card. And...Yea, I got pulled over."

"We will get back to Brenna. I think you better explain why and how you got pulled over."

"Well, crap...Okay. I felt incredible from my first day and excited about my upcoming date with you. So I had the music loud, and I was jammin'. I got lost in the moment. The next thing I saw was the dreaded red and blue lights. When the officer came to the door, I knew I was in deep shit because it was Brad," Abbey explained.

"So you were speeding?" he asked.

"Yes. I was. I know it wasn't much, but I was going seven over the limit. Plus, I know it was double wrong because I wasn't thinking and put myself at risk. I am sorry. I have vowed it won't happen again."

"I am not happy that you put yourself at risk. But I am so glad you told me yourself. Usually, you would deserve punishment for putting yourself in danger, but I also know you are new to all of this. So I would say no discipline is needed because you learned your lesson."

"Before you settle on that decision, I need to tell you the rest of it. I am telling you about it because Brad called James and told him what had happened. James told me I had until morning to tell you about it," Abbey said nervously.

"You still told me. Next time, I expect you to call and tell me on your own. Now no more dwelling on that. What did the card say from Brenna?"

"Brenna?" she asked.

"Brenna would be Mistress Ravan."

"Oh...Wait," she said as she quickly dug into her purse and handed the card to ZayShawn.

He read the card and returned it to Abbey just as their dinner arrived. They made small talk as they ate and discovered they had a lot in common. ZayShawn watched Abbey push around her salad; he knew something was bothering her.

"Abbey, what is swimming around that beautiful mind of yours?"

"I have questions, but I am afraid of the answers."

"Well, ask your questions, and we will figure out your answers together."

"Okay...If this works out. How will our relationship work?"

"I want a full-time submissive. But I will tweak my demands to make my submissive happy."

"That is what I was afraid of. ZayShawn, I don't think I will ever be able to be a full-time submissive. I am afraid if I say yes to that, I will lose myself to make someone else happy."

"Let me clear some things up for you. When I say a full-time submissive, I mean she will wear my collar full-time to show my ownership. She will respect me in the community by calling me Sir. When we play, she will call me Daddy. But I don't expect her to call me Sir or Daddy if we are at home. I am just ZayShawn, babe, baby, hun, or anything else she wants to call me. I will be a happy man if she also follows the rules of a submissive when she is with or without me. I don't expect her to kneel and wait for me to come home from work. My submissive will always have the freedom to be herself," he explained.

The smile that bloomed on Abbey's face lit up the room, and she ate once again.

Chapter 14

When they finished eating, ZayShawn stood and held his hand out for Abbey to take. When they started walking, his hand went to her lower back. Abbey was enjoying the feeling of his hand there. He nodded at the Maitre D on the way out.

"Um...Don't we need to pay?" asked a confused Abbey.

"I'm a member here. They will bill me," he explained.

"Cool."

After they were back in the car, ZayShawn took her on a city tour. He showed her where he worked, and when he pulled into his parent's driveway, she asked, "Who lives here?"

"My parents do," he said with a devilish grin.

She focused on the guest house when they drove past the huge house.

"Is this where you live?" she asked.

"Yes. I plan on buying a house when the time is right, but until then, this fits me. I come and go as I wish, and it is private."

She smiled and said, "I like it. Remember, when you are ready to buy a house, you know an amazing realtor."

Abbey waited for ZayShawn to open her door and help her out of the car. When he unlocked the entrance to the house, he said, "Alexa, lights."

As the lights in the living room turned on, she smiled to see he was a clean freak like her.

"Wait right here. I will be right back," he told her.

"Okay, Babe."

Abbey wandered around his living room, looking at family pictures waiting for him to return. She stopped and picked up a picture of a small boy and a beautiful black woman in the picture. He startled her when he reached around her, took the photo, and said, "That is me and my mom. I don't have many pictures of us together. But I am happy with the ones that I have. But I have Faye. She is amazing. She raised us boys as if we were her own."

"Does Faye have any kids?"

"Yes, she has a daughter; her name is Lizzy. We don't get to see her very often. She lives in Italy with her husband."

ZayShawn handed Abbey a glass of Crown apple and Sprite, then sat the picture back on the shelf.

"Let me give you the grand tour," he said, offering his hand.

Without hesitation, Abbey linked her fingers with his and went with him. When they entered the hallway, he said, "I know you are still deciding if this life is for you, but I still want to show you my playroom."

Abbey's muscles started quivering with excitement. When he opened the door, she walked in. She turned in a circle, looking at everything. ZayShawn watched her take in her surroundings. When she walked deeper into the room, he asked, "What do you think?"

"It is a little intimidating," she said, looking at the wall of leather cuffs.

"If you are not ready to play here, we can wait," he said softly.

"I trust you. I have one question. How many submissives have you played with in here?"

"You will be the first and hopefully the last. I finished this room last night," he said, walking up behind her.

"Is this the only room we will have sex in?" she asked quietly.

"Abbey, baby, look at me," he said, turning her around to face him.

When she looked up at him, he stroked her cheek and said, "I plan to make love to you all over the place. Just because we are in a D/S lifestyle doesn't mean we are not making love. There will be sometimes I will make slow sweet love to you in our bed, vanilla style. Sometimes we will be in our playroom, and I fuck the shit out of you hard and rough."

"Don't you think it is a little soon to be talking about love?" she asked quietly, as her heart pounded.

"Abbey, I am talking about our future. I already have strong feelings developing for you. It scares the shit out of me," he said quietly as he rested his forehead on hers.

When ZayShawn was quiet, she followed her instincts; she lifted her head and pressed her lips to his. ZayShawn wrapped his arms around her and pulled her close. When he broke the kiss, he whispered, "Do you want to play?"

When she nodded yes, he grinned.

"I want you to undress and kneel on the mat, waiting for my return. Do you understand, Beauty?" he commanded.

"Yes, Daddy."

He kissed her softly and left the room. Abbey quickly undressed. After folding her dress, she placed her clothing on a chair. She remembered he liked her hair braided, so she took down her hair. Then, after putting it in a single braid, she pulled a hair tie from her purse to secure it. Abbey knelt on the mat. Then remembered what James' subs looked like when they were waiting for him. So she placed her hands on her legs, palms up, and looked down at her lap.

When he returned, he stood behind her, and at the sight of her, a low growl escaped his chest, making her quiver.

"Beauty, stand and serve your Daddy," he commanded.

Abbey rocked on her heels and stood. When she turned around, seeing him made her weak in the knees. He had untied his dreads. They now hung, framing his face. He was chest bare, and she noticed the firefighter symbol tattooed on his right upper arm. He was wearing dark blue basketball shorts, and she could tell he was naked underneath, and his feet were bare.

"Are you ready to push some of your limits and play with something new?"

"Yes, Daddy."

"What kind of bondage would you like to try tonight?"

"I can pick?"

"Yes, Beauty. You may pick anything except leather cuffs."

"May I ask why?"

"Because I want to help you grow. If you only use leather cuffs, how will you know what other restraints feel like?"

Abbey nodded and went to the wall of restraints; there were metal handcuffs, zip ties, masking tape, ribbon, lace, and rope.

"Can we try the rope tonight, Daddy?" she asked.

"Yes, Beauty," he said, taking it off the wall. "I would also like you to try nipple clamps and some anal play. I understand butt plugs and anal sex are a hard limit for now. I want to try something. If you don't like it, we will never bring the subject up again. Are you willing to try?"

"I guess," she said, unsure.

"Good Girl," he praised.

ZayShawn stood next to a table that had cuffs on the bottom of the legs and padded leather on the top.

"Come here, Beauty; I want you to face the table, bend at the waist, and lay only the top of your beautiful body down."

When she did what he asked, he laid the rope on her back and knelt, cuffing her ankles to the table. He then stood and secured her hands behind her back.

"Color, Beauty."

"Green."

"Good girl. I could stand here and look at you for hours," he growled and bit her hip, making her squeak.

"Did you like that?"

"Yes, Daddy."

"Would you like me to do it again?"

"Oh, yes, Daddy, please," she purred.

ZayShawn smacked the apple of her ass, and when she cried out, he bit the other hip, making her moan.

"Did you like the spanking?"

"Mmm, Yes, Daddy."

"Would you like another?"

"Yes, Daddy."

This time when he started her spanking, he didn't stop to check with her, trusting her that if it became too much, she would call her safe word. After each smack, he would rub her ass and play with her clit. After five smacks, she was panting and was so wet he could smell it. He removed his shorts and stood behind her. He placed the head of his hard cock at the entrance of her wet pussy and gripped the rope between her bound wrist. With one push, he bottomed out, making Abbey scream, "Yes, Daddy." ZayShawn slowly pulled out to do it again. When ZayShawn started moving, he steadied himself at a medium pace and rolled his hips. He covered his thumb in her juices, and when she was almost ready to cum, he pushed his thumb into her tight rosebud. As soon as his thumb was in her ass Abbey violently came as she screamed. He carefully removed his thumb and slowly pulled his cock out of her.

He quickly unbound her hands and feet, then picked her up and carried her to the bed. After he laid her down, he collected his next set of props. When he returned, he bound her wrists in leather cuffs and hooked her hands to the headboard.

"I thought you said no leather cuffs tonight, Daddy?" she asked, smiling.

"I said you couldn't choose leather cuffs," he smiled back.

ZayShawn showed Abbey a set of nipple clamps shaped like a flower, with a chain connecting them.

"Beauty, these nipple clamps have a bite. And every time I tug on the chain, their bite gets harder. Are you still wanting to try them?"

Abbey bit her lip and nodded. She watched as he attached each one of them. When they were connected, he gave the chain a little tug. Abbey moaned while she arched her back while pulling on her restraints. He settled between her legs, and while pushing himself back inside her, he gave the chain a little tug. He growled when she tried to close her eyes and said, "Your eyes will always stay open and on me. Understood?"

"Yes, Daddy," she moaned.

"Beauty, you may not cum until I tell you to."

"Yes, Daddy," she cried between moans.

ZayShawn picked up his pace, and he placed one hand next to her head when he was on the edge of cumming. He leaned down and kissed Abbey. When he broke the kiss, he gripped the chain and growled, "Cum for Daddy."

When he felt her pussy quivering, he gave one hard tug on the chain, detaching the nipple clamps. When Abbey came, her vision went white, pushing her over the edge into subspace. ZayShawn rested his forehead on hers as he emptied himself inside of her. For the first time, Abbey came so hard she left a lake in the center of the bed.

When ZayShawn saw how far into subspace Abbey was flying, he cleaned her up and carried her to his bed. After cleaning himself, he crawled into bed beside Abbey and pulled her close. He placed her on his chest and softly stroked her back until he fell asleep.

Abbey woke a few hours later in a dark room, and once again, ZayShawn was her pillow. He tightened his arm around her when she moved, making her feel wanted and safe. Abbey enjoyed laying in ZayShawn's arms, but now she had to pee. She lifted her head to see if he was awake. His eyes were closed, but his sexy voice broke the silence. "Baby, are you okay?"

"Yes, everything is fine," she answered.

"That was a free one. The next time you lie to me, you will be punished. Now I can feel your eyes on me. What is wrong?"

"Noting is wrong; I just need to use the bathroom."

Saying nothing, he turned on the bedside lamp so she could leave the bed safely. It took a minute for Abbey's eyes to adjust to the lighting. She climbed out of bed and dashed to the bathroom when she could see. When he heard the toilet flush, he said, "Hurry, woman, I am getting lonely here." Abbey washed her hands and returned to the bed, facing him on her side.

"What did you think about tonight?" he asked, turning on his side.

"I enjoyed myself. I was scared at first, but in the end, I liked it."

"Good, I am glad. Now come here, woman. I am not done with you yet," he said, pulling her under him.

"Oh, really…" was the only thing she could get out before he covered her lips with his. Now that her hands were free, she did what she had wanted to do from the first time their eyes met. Abbey touched him everywhere she could reach; then she put her hand in his dreads. When he broke the kiss, he moved over to her shoulder. After kissing the nape of her neck, he sank his teeth in, making her moan softly. He moved his way down, worshipping every inch of her body his lips and hands touched. When he reached her breast, he bit down on her nipple and gave it a little pull. Then he continued his way south. He bit her inner thigh, making her body jump. He placed her legs over his shoulders and locked her in place with his arms. ZayShawn teased her by lightly licking her pussy lips. Then he buried his face in her wet pussy, teasing her clit with his tongue. When she was ready to cum, he softly bit her clit, making her fist her hands in his dreads, and pushed her over the edge. When her legs stopped trembling, he crawled up the bed and rested on his elbows. As he pushed into her, he kissed her softly. ZayShawn's pace was slow and sweet. After Abbey came again, he sat on his knees and pulled her up. "Wrap your legs around me, baby." Abbey did as instructed, and ZayShawn used his powerful arm to move her up and down on his cock.

"Baby, cum for me again," he whispered.

Her body responded to his demands, and she exploded again. ZayShawn was close to coming himself, so he switched positions. He tapped her on the ass and said, "I want you on all fours." Abbey was quick to comply. When she was on all fours, he wrapped her braid around his hand and pulled. When she moaned, he smacked her ass and shoved his cock back into her before the sting faded. The pace ZayShawn chose was fast and rough. When he felt himself building, he growled, "Come for me one more time, baby."

Once again, Abbey came screaming as ZayShawn emptied himself into her as her pussy milked him dry. When they came down from their orgasms, they collapsed on the bed. ZayShawn rolled to the side and pulled Abbey to his side.

"Abbey, will you stay the night with me? I will take you home in the morning to get ready for work. Then I will drive you to the office," he asked, kissing the top of her head.

"Yes, I will stay," she said, snuggling in.

ZayShawn turned off the light and started stroking her back softly. It wasn't long before she was sleeping. Just as he was dozing off, he swore he heard her say, "I think I am falling in love with you, and it scares the shit out of me. Please don't hurt me."

"I know I'm falling for you. Sweet Dreams, my beautiful Angel."

Chapter 15

The sound of the alarm made Abbey stir, waking ZayShawn.

"Good Morning, Baby," he said, rubbing her back.

"Mornin'."

ZayShawn slipped out of bed and started the shower. When it was up to temp, he returned to the bedroom, pulled the covers off Abbey, and picked her up, making her grumble. When she started squirming, he tossed her over his shoulder and stalked to the bathroom straight into the shower, letting the spray hit her face.

"Hey, what the fuck are you doing? Put me down. Listen, you fuck twit, if you don't put me down and get the fucking water out of my face, I am going to fucking whoop your ass," she sputtered.

When ZayShawn put her down, he laughed, "Aww come on, Baby. It's just a little water. A little water never hurt anyone."

She turned to let him have it, and her anger melted. He had that panty-dropping smile plastered on his face.

"You know you are lucky."

"Why am I lucky?"

"Because you're sexy, and I like your smile."

He laughed as he pumped some pale liquid into his hands. He pulled her close and stared, massaging it into her hair.

"What are you putting in my hair?"

"UH. Shampoo...what else would it be?"

"Why do you have white girl shampoo in your shower?"

"I asked James what you use and picked it up yesterday. Satisfied worry wort?"

"Oh shut up, ass."

"Keep that up, and I will label you as a brat. It might be fun being a brat tamer."

"No, you want to see a brat? I feel sorry for whoever becomes Ava's Dom. That bitch is a true brat. I bet her first week with him, she won't be able to sit down for a year."

"That's not very nice."

"Do you want me to be nice or tell the truth?"

"The truth... always the truth."

"That is one thing you will never have to worry about with me. I may be blunt and come off cold sometimes, but I don't lie," she said, looking up at him.

"That is the same for me. You will always get honesty."

Abbey raised to her toes and kissed him softly. Knowing they did not have time for what he wanted to do, they finished showering.

"Stay right here," he said after shutting off the water.

He pulled a towel off the rack and wrapped it around his waist. He grabbed a second towel and handed it to Abbey. When they returned to the bedroom, he went to his dresser and opened the top drawer. He grabbed a pair of boxers and a beater.

"You can take these home with you. If you miss me when I work nights, you can wear them."

Abbey's heart warmed by the gift. She took the clothes and tossed them on the bed. Abbey then wrapped her arms around his neck and said, "Thank you."

After ZayShawn dropped Abbey off at the office, he made an important phone call. If the call went well, his next stop would be to ask for some much-needed time off.

After the phone started ringing, it seemed to take forever for Terrance to answer.

Terrance: What the fuck, man? This better be important.

ZayShawn: "I know you just started your three-week Vay-cay last night, but I have a big favor to ask."

Terrance: "Where's the body?"

ZayShawn: "What?"

Terrance: "There must be a body you want me to help hide. Because you are calling me at seven am on my VACATION."

ZayShawn: "No, Dick head. I want you to teach me, Kinbaku."

Terrance: "What? Why now? I tried to teach you a couple of years ago."

ZayShawn: "Because I think Abbey is a rope bunny. When we were talking, she said it interested her."

Terrance: "And?"

ZayShawn: "Are you going to teach me or what? If you don't, I will find someone else to."

Terrance: "Yes. Be here at two. We will start your lessons today."

Before he could say thank you, Terrance hung up. Next, he drove across town to talk with the fire chief.

When he arrived at City Hall, he decided on the stairs instead of waiting in line for the elevators. The haze from lack of sleep wore off when he reached the fifth floor. He smiled at the chief's secretary and approached her desk.

"Good Morning, Jewels. Is the chief in?"

"Good Morning to you, too, Marshal. Yes, he is. Did you need to see him?"

"Yes, if he has time."

"You are in luck; he has twenty minutes before his next meeting."

"Thank you, Jewels."

Jewels nodded as she picked up her phone and murmured. She returned the phone to the base and said, "You can go right in."

ZayShawn nodded and walked through the door.

"Hello, Mr. Williams," the chief said with a smile.

"Mr. Williams? Really Uncle Jack?" ZayShawn said, sitting down.

"Well, I have to be professional sometimes," he laughed. "So, what brings you into my office on your day off?"

"Well, you know all that vacation time I have racked up? I need to cash in some of it."

"Holy fuck, the world must be ending. ZayShawn Williams is asking for some time off. How much do you want to take?" Jack asked.

"Well, I have six months saved up. I think I will cash in three months. If you can swing it."

"Yeah, I can swing it. What is so important that you want three months off?"

"I am getting ready to take some classes, and I have some things I need to put in motion for my future?"

"So, nephew, does this have anything to do with the blue-haired beauty that walked into the club a few nights ago?"

"Maybe..."

"Fuck...Have you even talked to her?"

"Yes, I'm not an idiot."

"Then tell me about her."

"First. Her name is Abbey. She is smart, beautiful, kind-hearted, and is very close to her brother."

"Does she even live in the lifestyle, son? How is her brother going to feel when he finds out some black man is tieing up his sister and then fucking the shit out of her?" asked Jack.

"Well, since you are being so nosey. She is new to the lifestyle, which is perfect because we can grow together. Trust me, her brother knows about my extracurricular activities. He had a fit when Abbey and her friends walked into the club," ZayShawn chuckled.

"Her brother is James Brewer?"

"That would be the one," he said with a smile.

"You know, if this goes wrong, you kicked a fucking hornet's nest," warned Jack.

"I know what I am doing. So, do I have the time off or not?" asked ZayShawn.

"Yes, now get the hell out of here, you crazy ass."

"Thank you, Jack."

ZayShawn waved to Jewels on his way out and took the stairs. He needed to make one more stop before heading to his brother's house.

ZayShawn drove across town to see James. He was about to honk when the gates swung open, allowing him to pull up to the house.

James greeted him at the door, "Come on in; I was just sitting down to eat. What brings you to my door? You know you are always welcome here. But I have a feeling this has to do with Abbey."

"Yes...well, and you," said ZayShawn.

"Come on in; we will talk about it over lunch," James offered.

He followed James through the house to the back patio. The table was filled with meat, cheese, and different fruits.

"Do you always eat like this for lunch?" ZayShawn asked.

"No, Star is trying to earn brownie points; she has been on punishment the past couple of days," James said, picking up a strawberry. "Now, what did you want to talk about?"

"I am falling in love with Abbey."

James sat back and studied the man that might be in his sister's life forever. While gathering his thoughts and emotions, he ate fruit and drank sweet tea. He knew the silence was making ZayShawn uneasy by the way he shifted in his seat.

"You just met her," James said quietly.

"Yes, I know. Abbey is the most remarkable person I have ever met."

"I know...she is my sister. If you are asking if you can run away with her and get married...The answer is NO!!!"

"No, marriage is a long way off. But I know I want to collar her. Plus, I wanted to discuss having you do a scene with us."

"I am not having sex with my sister!"

"Dear god, hell no! That is not what I am asking. I want to show her that Fire Play is safe and doesn't hurt. You were the one that taught me how to use the bullwhip. I would like you to teach me Fire Play if she likes it. James, I came to you because you are a master at Fire Play," ZayShawn explained.

"I will say yes on the Fire Play. We will do it at Fetish. Keep this to yourself. If she knows that this is the plan, she will bolt. One, because fire makes her nervous, and two, because I will be in the scene with you two. Now on the business of collaring her. Come back to me in a few months, and we can discuss it."

"When would you be available to do the scene?" ZayShawn asked.

"Tonight is the only night I have available for a few months."

"Tonight sounds great. I just took three months off work. So, tonight is perfect."

"Why did you take three months off?"

"I am taking Kinbaku classes from Terrance. It interests Abbey, and she loves bondage. So, I want to do this for her."

"Dude, you are falling. I remember when your brother got his certificate and wanted to teach you. Your exact words were, 'I don't need to play with rope to make my submissive happy. If she wants to play with rope, I will remind her how much fun leather is.' So it took a blue-haired vixen to walk into your life."

"No, you ass, it took a good woman to make me fall in love."

Chapter 16

A bbey had been working all morning, emailing the offers she had received from yesterday's open houses. As she hit send on the last one, there was a knock at her door.

"Yes," Abbey said without looking up.

"You have a delivery, Ms. Abbey."

"Delivery?"

"Yes, Ms. Abbey," her assistant said, holding a medium box.

Abbey's eyes lit up, and the butterflies fluttered in her stomach as she stood and took the box. Her hands trembled because this box matched the last two boxes she had received. She closed the door and set the box on her desk. She looked at the black box with the massive red bow. Taking a deep breath, she untied the bow and lifted the lid off the box. She picked up the note card and read:

Baby Girl.

Your presence is required to join me tonight at Fetish. This is the outfit you are required to wear. I've listed the rest of the requirements for your ensemble below.

1. You are to wear no undergarments. This means NO bra and NO panties.

2. Your hair must be braided into a tight tail with no flyaways. NO hairspray, only gel.

3. No perfume or scented lotion.

4. If you wear earrings, only hoops.

5. You can wear your make-up any way you want. Use setting powder in place of spray.

Make sure you are ready to walk out of work at five pm. That way, you can come home to shower and prepare to be at the club at seven pm. Ava will be your ride home.

I look forward to seeing you tonight.

Sir James

When Abbey pulled open the tissue paper and looked at what was in the box, she sat down and said, "OH SHIT!"

Abbey looked at her watch and saw that it was three-thirty pm. Excited about tonight, she had difficulty focusing on the last part of her day. Every time she looked at the clock, it seemed only five minutes had passed. When her computer signaled that she had an incoming email, she jumped at it. Abbey yelled, scaring everyone in the office.

"Whooo hooo."

A few coworkers approached her office door and asked, "Is everything okay?"

"Yes, everything is wonderful! I just sold my first house," she said, dancing happily.

"Congratulations. What house?" asked Gennie.

"Hold on, let me check," she said, looking at her computer. "Ummm, The Baker's residence."

"No way...I have been trying to sell that house for over a year. What did it sell for?" Gennie asked.

"Nine hundred and fifty thousand," Abbey said proudly.

"Can someone please tell me where Ms. Abbey Brown's office is?" They heard someone call from the front.

She recognized her bestie's voice and yelled, "Back here, Ava!"

When Ava rounded the corner, all Abbey could do was smile. Ava had her wild, curly red hair free of bands. Even wearing a tee shirt, cut-off shorts, and flat tennies, she still looked like a supermodel.

"Abbs, are you ready to go? It is five after five. I am not getting hollered at if you are late. I love James, but when he is cross, he is something else. Trust me; I have learned my lesson."

"Yes, I just need to grab my bag and this box, and I am ready to go. I will see you, ladies, in the morning," Abbey said, walking to the front of the office.

Abbey and Ava walked into the club at seven on the dot. ZayShawn had his back to the entrance and knew when Abbey walked in. He turned to greet her with a smile, but his mouth went slack at her outfit.

"Bro...Are you going to let her dress like that?" asked Terrance.

"He has no choice. I am the one that bought her that outfit, and she looks hot," James said, walking off to greet his girls.

"I am going to kill James," ZayShawn growled.

"Brother, control yourself. You have no say-so. Abbey is not your collared submissive yet," Terrance reminded him.

"Yet is the key word, brother. That will change very soon," he said as he finished the last of the crown in his glass.

"What is the problem, son?" LaMarkus asked.

"The way Abbey is dressed is the problem," he growled.

LaMarkus turned and looked at Abbey and shook his head. Abbey was wearing a black leather bra with leather latticework pants and knee-high boots.

When James, Abbey, and Ava joined the rest of the group, Abbey could feel the tension building between James and ZayShawn.

"James, we need to have some words be for we get on stage," ZayShawn growled.

James rocked back on his heels and smiled sadistically. "Yes, I believe we do."

"What is going on?" asked Abbey.

"Don't worry, Abbey, you will be there to hear every word," ZayShawn said as he wrapped an arm around her waist, pulling her close.

"Well, we have ten minutes before we need to be on stage, so let's get on with this," James said.

When the guys started walking off, Abbey looked back at Ava.

"Get going, and don't let them kill each other," Ava said, shooing her off.

Abbey walked around the curtain just in time to witness ZayShawn's fist meet James' jaw.

"What the hell is going on? Why the fuck did you hit him?" Abbey said, checking James' cheek.

"Don't baby him; he is not innocent. He had you dressed like that tonight because I told him earlier I wanted to offer you a collar and that I was falling in love with you," ZayShawn growled with his fist still clenched.

"James, is that true?" she said, backing away.

"Yes, but before you go psycho, listen to me. First, I am the Dom that holds the key to your protection collar. I need to know the Dom that collars you will take care of you as he should. As your brother, this man came to me only days after meeting you and told me he is falling in love with you. Third, I dressed her like this because of the scene we are performing," James explained.

"James, was this the only outfit that would have worked for the scene tonight?" Abbey asked.

"Well...No. I picked it because you look hot, and knew it would annoy ZayShawn. So I am sorry for my part in the shenanigans. I love you, Abbey, and I only want the best for you."

"James Charles Brewer. What you did to ZayShawn was unfair. Putting me between the men I love is not fair. It touches my heart. You want only the best for me and want to shield me from anything that would hurt me. James, you know you are my world. My heart is big enough to love more than one person with my whole being. So, as your sister, please be nice to ZayShawn. As the Dom that is vetting, Sir, you have the right to ensure I will be taken care of. Now boys, shake hands and makeup," Abbey demanded.

"You know, for a sub, you are awful brave talking to two Doms like this," James said, smirking.

"Oh, and I should be free from punishment because of yall's shenanigans."

"You will always get a free pass when standing up for yourself or someone you love, as long as it is done respectfully," ZayShawn said, pulling her close.

"Let's go; we have a scene to perform," James said, smiling.

"Wait, what? Why? Who? Umm, No," stammered Abbey.

"Beauty, this is a command."

Abbey bowed her head and said, "Yes, Sir."

She shook from fear as she stood on stage, not because it was her brother. It was because she was on stage with one of the most respected Doms in the community.

Chapter 17

When the lighting dimmed in the club, Abbey knew something differed from the last. Abbey remembered how Daddy wanted her to wait for him. So going on her instincts, she knelt on the mat and placed her hands on her lap, palms up and head bowed. She listened to ZayShawn and James move around the stage, setting up the scene. When they were done, they joined Abbey at the front of the stage, standing on each side of her.

"Hello, everyone. Twice a month, we put on a show here at Fetish. Normally, I would scene with my subs with one other Dom. But tonight, I am using the show to teach a Dom a new technique on his submissive. I will ask all of you to please keep the noise down. She is a new submissive and new to this type of play. If there is a lot of noise, it will distract her from our commands and the sound of our voices. So, please sit back and enjoy the show," announced James.

James touched Abbey's head and said, "Tonight, you will call me Master. I will call you Baby Girl. Do you understand?"

Abbey swallowed and said, "Yes, Master."

"Good Girl," James said with pride.

"Do you remember the rules, Beauty?"

"Yes, Daddy,"

"That's my Good Girl," ZayShawn said, standing a little taller.

"Baby Girl, tonight we are going to play with fire."

James watched as Abbey's body jerked when she found out what the scene was.

"Beauty, I want you to stand and remove all of your clothing," ZayShawn commanded.

Without hesitation, Abbey rocked on her heels and stood. Piece by piece, she made herself bare for all to see.

"Baby Girl, come lay face down on the table," James commanded.

Abbey approached the table, and as soon as she was going to lift herself up, she felt ZayShawn's hands on her hips. He lifted her onto the table and helped her lay down.

"Relax, Beauty," ZayShawn soothed.

"Yes, Daddy."

"Baby Girl, to help you relax, we will flog you. Before you can get flogged, you must be bound to the table. Do you understand?"

"Yes, Master."

"Good Girl."

James and ZayShawn quickly bound her hands and legs to the table. Then James pressed play on the mp3 player; Beyond The Veil by Lindsey String filled the club. James and ZayShawn alternated between each other, landing blows with the leather floggers to the beat of the music. Abbey's body relaxed with each strike from the floggers.

"Color, Baby Girl."

"Green, Master," she purred.

"Good Girl."

As ZayShawn continued flogging, James got the supplies for Fire Play. When he was ready, he gave ZayShawn tongs, one wet and one on fire. Together, the Doms drew pictures on Abbey's back with the wet cotton balls, then set it on fire. The flames seem to dance to the beat of the music. She moaned from the warmth of the flames each time the fire touched Abbey's back. As the song changed, they quickly unbound her and helped her to her back. Once again, they drew patterns on her breasts, stomach, legs, and even the bottoms of her feet. ZayShawn drew the last design.

Before setting it on fire, he said, "Beauty, this last picture is for you." Then, he touched the flame, setting the picture on fire, revealing a heart.

"Baby Girl, I will now leave you with your Dom. You were a very Good Girl tonight. You have filled me with pride," James said as he bent down and kissed her forehead. Never noticing what he said made Abbey's eyes fill with tears.

"ZayShawn, it has been a pleasure helping you tonight," James said as he held his hand out.

When ZayShawn gripped his hand to shake, James tightened his grip and said, "You have my blessing when you two are ready."

ZayShawn felt a lump in his throat and couldn't speak, so he nodded at James and watched him walk off stage.

ZayShawn was torn. He didn't want to give a piece of himself and Abbey to the community, but he also needed them to see the bond they already had made. So he vowed this would be the only time he publicly shared her.

"Beauty, are you ready to play?"

"Yes, Daddy."

"Then let's play, my Good Girl."

ZayShawn helped Abbey off the table and led her to a padded bench.

"Wait here," he commanded.

ZayShawn went to his bag and pulled out a pair of leather cuffs. He returned to Abbey, and she held out her wrist. After he buckled them, he said, "Look at the cuffs."

Abbey's eyes filled with excitement. The black leather cuffs said Daddy's good girl with a red rose. Abbey looked up into ZayShawn's eyes, and she smiled.

"Yes, Beauty, these are for you. They will come with us every time we scene, or we will use them in our playroom. Do you like them?"

"Oh yes, Daddy. I love them. Thank you."

"You're welcome. Now I want you to straddle the bench like you were riding me."

When Abbey was in place, he moved to the front of the bench and clipped her cuffs to the legs of the bench.

"Beauty, do you know what this bench is called?"

"No, Daddy. What is it?"

"This is a spanking bench. Would you like me to paddle your sexy pink ass?"

"Yes, Daddy. Please."

"Would you like your spanking with my hand or the paddle?"

"Whatever you like, Daddy?"

"Oh, with that response, I think I will use my hand."

Abbey purred under ZayShawn's touch as he rubbed her right ass cheek. ZayShawn picked up the rhythm after each swat; he would rub her ass, making the sting vibrate throughout her body. When every cry came from a swat, she would moan when he rubbed her tender ass. When Abbey's ass was rose pink, she heard him unzip his jeans.

"Beauty, are you ready for me?"

"Yes, Daddy," she moaned.

He gripped her hips and slid her body down the bench, stretching her arms, and he helped place her feet on the floor.

"Beauty, you are my precious Angel, but tonight I am going to fuck you like a dirty slut."

Without reservation, he entered her greedy, wet pussy with one stroke, causing Abbey to scream in ecstasy. Every time ZayShawn would pull out, he would smack Abbey's ass making her scream and pant. When he was close to coming, he yelled, "Come for me, Beauty."

Her body responded to his command; ZayShawn quickly followed, letting out a primal growl when he came. When he pulled out of her, she went limp. He turned his head and nodded at the bouncer, and he closed the curtain.

"Wait right here, baby, and I will take care of you," he said softly.

ZayShawn zipped his pants and unbound Abbey from the bench. When he lifted her in his arms, he kissed her softly. When he pulled back, he noticed she was crying. Scared that he had hurt her, he sat on the couch and held her close.

"Baby, I am so sorry if I hurt you."

"You didn't hurt me, ZayShawn."

"Then why are you crying?"

"Because my heart is overfilled."

"Baby, please explain," he pleaded.

"I know it is so soon, but I love you, ZayShawn. How I feel scares me. It would destroy me if you left or found a different submissive," she sniffled.

"Abbey, I love you, too. I am not going anywhere. You are my first and last submissive. I told you I wanted a love that would last like my dad and Faye. I know I have found that in you. We can still take our time. Just know Abbey Brown. You are mine."

Abbey sat up and wrapped her arms and legs around ZayShawn and held on tight.

Chapter 18

Over the next few months, Abbey worked on building her career and spending time with ZayShawn at his house and at Fetish. She has enjoyed ZayShawn being on vacation. Sometimes he would show up and take her to lunch. On others, she would walk out of work to find him outside waiting for her.

The first house she sold would close in a few days. The company owner told Abbey they would handle the closing on the home themselves, even though she would still get the commission. Later in the week, Abbey and the girls were going shopping for the masked party at Fetish. James said it was mandatory that his girls were there. Abbey was also excited that she and the girls were starting classes with Mistress Ravan next week. Abbey still wondered where ZayShawn was disappearing to a few days a week.

He told her to be patient and that she will find out. Although she hated waiting, she remained submissive and complied with his command.

On the day of the party at Fetish, ZayShawn ran some last-minute errands. He had his last class at two and his suit to pick before five. He felt like a high school teenager. He couldn't wait to see Abbey. She told him her outfit was teal and black, so he got his suit to match. As he pulled into traffic, his phone rang.

ZayShawn: "Hello?"

James: "Hey, have you talked to Abbey?"

ZayShawn: "Not since lunch. What's up?"

James: "Nothing really, just girl chatter. I have the halfway house for wayward submissives, remember?"

ZayShawn: "Dude, you are my hero."

James: "Shut the fuck up. You do not know what I deal with on a day-to-day basis."

ZayShawn: "Sorry, man."

James: "You know I have to ask. Are you sure you are ready for tonight?"

ZayShawn: "Yes, I was ready three months ago."

James: "Just wanted to make sure. The item you had me order came in. I will bring it to the club tonight."

ZayShawn: "Thanks, man."

James: "Not a problem. You earned it. I will see you tonight...Later."

ZayShawn: "Later."

Abbey felt like someone had pushed the fast-forward button on a remote. Whenever Abbey thought she could catch her breath, her boss would pull her in the opposite direction. By one-thirty, she was ready for a nap.

"Ready for coffee?" Gennie asked.

"Can we pretend we are in kindergarten just for today?" Abbey pouted.

"Why?"

"I need a damn nap," she said, laying her head on her desk.

"If you want coffee, we need to go now. Don't forget you need to pull the file for the Baker closing today at two. So come on. Abbey, please, I need caffeine," Gennie whined while she acted like she was fading away.

Abbey chuckled, "Come on...we don't need your skinny ass fading away."

As Abbey and ZayShawn were caught in the whirlwind of their day. James, Ava, Sara, and Hannah worked with LaMarkus and Faye on the last-minute party touches.

"Why isn't my son here helping since this is his damn party?" LaMarkus asked.

"Because he is taking care of last-minute things himself," James grinned.

"What last-minute things?" asked Ava.

"That would be none-yah. Now be a good girl and finish setting up the tables," James commanded.

"Yes, Sir," pouted Ava.

"Sir, who is picking up Abbey from work?" Sara asked.

"Didn't she take the car?"

"Nope, I dropped her off on the way to my photo shoot," answered Ava.

"Well fuck...okay, you girls go pick her up. That way, you all can get ready together. I will call my flower girls in. They can help finish up."

As the girls gathered their stuff to leave, Sara's mood plummeted to the pits of hell.

"What the hell rained on your sunshine?" asked Hannah.

"That man right there. He is like a cheese grater on my nerves," snarled Sara.

"Are you still sour Mr. Terry punished you for what you did wrong?" Ava asked.

"Bitch, shut the fuck up...Nobody asked you to open your mouth," Sara said, stomping off.

The girls piled in the car and zoomed across town to pick up their bestie. Abbey was closing her office down as the girls arrived; when Abbey saw her girls, her heart swelled.

"Let's go; we have a party to get ready for," Ava said, dancing.

"Well, let's go then...Whoa, what's wrong with Sara? Who pissed in her cornflakes?" asked Abbey.

"Terrance walked into the club and smiled at her," Hannah said, grinning.

"What is wrong with him?"

"She is still butt hurt she got spanked," Ava laughed.

"You all are bitches...Just shut the fuck up and let's go," Sara said, turning and walking out of the building.

The girls took advantage of James leaving them unattended during the day. Abbey found the remote to the radio and synced her iPhone, and hit play on her iTunes playlist. Nasty by Lil Duval was the first song that played. Just like in their college days, Abbey turned the music to blasting, and the girls had a blast dancing while getting ready for a new adventure that awaited them tonight.

The girls decided on the same outfit, just different colors. To honor James, they decided the color of their outfits would match the keys around his neck. They were wearing two-piece dresses. The top was a tube top with black clasps; the bottom was a low-hanging tube skirt with a slit up to the hip. They wore matching black pumps. They left their hair free of clips and bands and did their make-up to match their outfits. Their simple black masks complimented their eyes.

James had ordered a limo to take the girls to the club. When they walked into Fetish, all eyes were on them. ZayShawn itched to be at Abbey's side. But out of respect for the community and for the Dom, that has her under protection, he had to wait for James to escort her in. Everyone watched as James kissed each one of his girls and then led them into the club. He led them over to the table where their friends were sitting.

ZayShawn snaked his arm around Abbey's waist and kissed her cheek.

"I can't wait until you are mine," he growled.

Abbey looked up at him and smiled; when she laid her head on his chest, ZayShawn nodded at his father. LaMarkus took the box James handed him and went to the center stage with a table. Before speaking, he placed the box on the table and faced the community.

"Hello, everyone; welcome to Fetish's first collaring ceremony. In this community, we thrive on supporting each other. So I ask you for that support tonight. Will James join me on stage, please?"

When James walked to the stage, Abbey whispered, "Is James taking a submissive?"

"Shh, Beauty...you will see," ZayShawn whispered back.

"I would like to thank everyone for coming. When I was new to Dallas LaMarkus and his beautiful submissive gave me a home here at Fetish. The love and support from this community helped me become who I am today. Three months ago, I called my childhood best friend and invited her and her friends to join me here in Dallas. The second night here, they followed me and found themselves inside the doors of Fetish. From that night, all four girls have stepped into the lifestyle that called to them. To keep them safe, I placed protection collars on my girls. I told them the only way the locks on their collars would unlock would be if they found a Dom/Domme or left the lifestyle. We will replace one of those collars tonight. Ms. Abbey Brown, come and join me."

Abbey jerked at hearing her name. She looked up at ZayShawn, and he said, "Go to him, Beauty."

Abbey walked with her head held high and stood next to James.

"Abbey, I have known you my whole life. You have grown into a beautiful person. I enjoyed watching you blossom under a Dom's guidance. You still have a lot to learn. You will never stop growing if you are open to new things. Are you willing to continue training once the protection collar is removed?"

"Yes, Sir."

"Then kneel before me," James commanded.

Abbey shook as she knelt in front of James when the sound of the lock seemed to echo when it released.

Abbey felt bare when the collar was removed. James held out his hand for Abbey to take. When she placed her hand in his, James helped her stand. James placed the collar on the table and took Abbey's face in his hands.

"I am so proud of you," James said as he softly kissed her cheek.

"Thank you, Sir," she said as her voice shook.

"Stand right here."

Unable to speak, she nodded.

"ZayShawn Williams, will you join us?"

Abbey's body vibrated as she watched as her future walked toward her.

"ZayShawn Williams, you asked for my permission to collar a submissive under my protection. Tonight I give you my blessing to claim her. If she agrees, the collaring ceremony will start."

ZayShawn turned to Abbey and said, "Abbey Brown, I love you. I want to claim you as mine. Are you willing to wear my collar?"

Abbey looked into ZayShawn's eyes as hers filled.

"It would be my honor to wear your collar," she said proudly.

ZayShawn turned and opened the box and took out a white gold collar with an Alexandrite shaped into a heart dangling in the front. The precious stone glittered when the light hit it. When Abbey saw the stone, she looked over at James; she knew by the smile on his face that he had helped ZayShawn pick out her collar.

"Abbey, I offer this collar to you as a symbol of my ownership of you. Do you accept?"

"Yes, I accept your collar as a symbol of your ownership over me, and I will wear it proudly for all to see."

"Then kneel before me to show your submission," ZayShawn commanded.

Abbey knelt and placed her hands on her lap, palms up, and her head bowed.

The white gold collar was cool on her skin; when the lock clicked closed, Abbey felt empowered that she now belonged to ZayShawn. When ZayShawn stood before Abbey, she took her submission one step further. She leaned forward and kissed the top of ZayShawn's feet. When she sat back up, he helped her stand.

"Abbey Brown, you now belong to me. You are my Angel," ZayShawn growled.

"Sir, I now belong to you," Abbey purred.

ZayShawn fisted a hand in her hair, tipped her head back, and crushed his mouth to hers.

Later in the night, ZayShawn led Abbey to his car and opened the door for her to climb in. Abbey felt complete for the first time in her life. She had her brother back and was now submissive to the man of her dreams. Abbey listened to the low music playing in the car and held onto ZayShawn's hand as he drove. Abbey recognized the part of town that ZayShawn was going through.

"Hey, the first house I sold is in this neighborhood. I was flying high that day. I sold the house and went on my first date with you," she said, smiling.

When he pulled into the driveway, she said, "This is the house!"

He was out of the car and opening her door before she could say anything else. ZayShawn held his hand out to her and said, "Come with me, Angel."

After she climbed out of the car, he shut the door and headed for the house's front door.

"Umm. Sir, Daddy, ZayShawn...I highly suggest we leave. I don't think the new owners will like us being here. Baby, please, I don't want to go to jail for trespassing," she pleaded.

"Baby, I don't think the new owners will mind," he said, unlocking the front door. "Come with me. I want to show you something."

Abbey knew she could trust ZayShawn, so she went with him willingly. He led her through the house and up the stairs. At the end of the hall, he told her to close her eyes. When her eyes were closed, he opened the door and walked to the center of the room.

"You can open your eyes now, Angel," he said softly.

When Abbey opened her eyes, she found herself in a BDSM playground.

"I don't understand."

"Go look around," he commanded.

Abbey walked around, looking at everything. On one of the walls, she noticed a set of cuffs next to a picture. Walking over, she picked up the cuffs and said, "No..." Then she looked at the picture. It was a certificate of completion for learning the art of Kinbaku for ZayShawn Williams. Abbey turned and looked at ZayShawn.

"Welcome home, Ms. Brown."

Abbey squealed, dropped the cuffs, then ran and jumped into ZayShawn's arms. ZayShawn could feel that Abbey was crying, and he said, "Why are you crying?"

"Because I am happy."

"So am I, baby...So am I. Tonight is the first night of the rest of our lives."

The End of the First Book of the Submissive's Club!

Collared

Xavier/Ava

~ Xavier~

Xavier sat at the end of the bar in his father's club, Fetish, sipping his crown and coke.

"Wonderful son that I have raised. When will you settle down and give me a daughter and grandkids?" Faye asked sweetly.

"Oh, come on, Faye, don't start this again. Talk to Terrance. He is the oldest," Xavier said, kissing her cheek.

"Fooey, I have given up on him. You and ZayShawn are my target," Faye said, leaning on the bar.

"Good luck. Your best bet will be with ZayShawn. I have no plans for settling down. It will have to be one hell of a woman to knock me off my feet for me to settle," he said with a shit-eating grin.

"Mark my words, son of mine...One day it will happen," she said, standing up.

"This looks like a serious talk. Anything I can help with?" asked LaMarkus.

"No, Daddy, all hope is lost...The children I slaved away to help raise refuse to give me daughters or grandchildren. I have washed my hands of them," she sniffed, pretending to pout.

"Oh, my beautiful Faye. If it will make you happy, I will write them out of the will," he said, pulling her close.

"What the Fuck, Dad?" Xavier whinnied, making them laugh.

"Seriously, son, why did you take all those classes to become a Dom if you never plan on collaring a sub?"

"Because I am a Dom. Why do I need to collar a sub when I can have all the fun I want here?"

"Watch it, boy...You are skating on the line of being labeled an unworthy Dom," warned LaMarkus.

"Why are you only telling me this? Terrance, don't have a sub," Xavier shot back.

LaMarkus slammed his fist on the bar, making the glasses rattle, and he growled, "He's not in here every night fucking a different sub. Don't forget, boy...This is my club, and I can blacklist you. So I advise you to clean up your act and quit acting like a spoiled teenage boy. Do I make myself clear?"

"Yes, Dad," Xavier said, looking down at the bar.

~Ava~

"What did she say?" Hannah asked Abbey.

"She needed help," Abbey answered.

"Nothing else?" Sara asked.

"NO! She sounded hurt, and the fucking phone went dead," Abbey yelled.

"Abbey, calm down. We need you to think. Did she tell you where she was headed?" asked Sara.

"She said she was heading to the campus library," Abbey said, feeling defeated.

"Then, that's where we will start. Come on," Hannah said, running off.

The girls found Ava curled in a ball under a bench in the campus square. Her clothes were ripped and bloody. The right side of her face was swollen, and her eye had swollen shut. She had red abrasions around her throat, wrist, and ankles, and her left arm looked broken. Blood and leaves matted her hair. When Abbey reached for Ava, she kicked out and screamed. Ava's foot connected with Abbey's right shoulder.

"Ava, honey, it's me, Abbey," she said, crying.

The haze lifted at hearing Abbey's voice. Ava said, "Abbey?"

"Yes, baby, it's me. Hannah and Sara are here, too. Come on, let us help you," Abbey soothed.

While Sara and Abbey helped Ava from under the bench, Hannah called the police. Abbey, Hannah, and Sara sat on the ground, making a protective circle around Ava until the police arrived.

Kitten Anderson

I am a 41-year-old true-life submissive. I have been collared and married to my Dom for 20+ years. I am an English Major. I love spending time with my family, salt-water fishing, and spending time on the beach. When I am not writing, you can find me curled up with a good book and a glass of wine.

Sunshine Anderson

When I was in high school, I wrote a book, but I never published it. I got the courage to publish a book when my sister, Kitten Anderson, asked me to co-author a series of books with her. Just to tell you a little about myself, I am 44 years old, and I am classified as a Switch. I was intrigued by the BDSM lifestyle from talking with my sister and reading books. I am a very family-oriented person. My kids and grandkids are my world. When my sister is not being a slave driver and working my fingers bloody, (Ha Ha). I love to spend time fishing in the Mississippi Sound, crafting, and spending time at family BBQs when my brother is playing king of the grill. I love to read, collect gnomes, and watch cheesy comedies on TV.

Sunshine & Kitten Anderson

BEST SELLING BDSM EROTICA AUTHORS

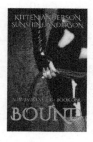

Abbey embarks on a new adventure with her high school friends after she gets a phone call from her best friend, James. After growing up in the small town of Middlesboro, Kentucky, Abbey has been craving a fresh start in life. After arriving in Dallas, she is enticed by the big city, and just down the road, a neon sign calls to her inner freak.

ZayShawn Willams, Fire Marshal for the Dallas Fire Department, is on the prowl for his new submissive. One night, sitting in his family's club, he watched a group of women walk in unattended. But the only one that caught his eye was the blue-haired vixen. Will he be able to tame her bratty ways?

Ava Walker is always looking for a new adventure, so when her best friend Abbey said she was moving to Dallas, her bags were the first to be packed. Ava was ready to put the small town of Middlesboro and the trauma she endured in her second year of college behind her.

Ava caught the eye of Xavier Williams the night she walked into Fetish. He had never been the one to want to settle down or collar a Sub, but since the night Ava walked into his Father's club, that was all he could think about. Xavier has decided he will do anything to make the smart-mouth red-headed bombshell his. Will Xavier win her heart and earn her trust? Or will the trauma from Ava's past stop him from collaring the woman of his dreams?

Faye Black runs a nightclub with her Dom, LaMarkus. She loves the life they have created, But now that her Step-sons are grown, she feels like something is missing. Little did she know that her life would be turned upside down when four unaccompanied women walked into Fetish.

LaMarkus Williams has raised three sons and owns a BDSM nightclub with his Submissive, Faye. His longtime friend Brenna Hayes comes to him with an opportunity that might make him rearrange his life. Will Faye stay and support him, or will she ask for the key to her collar?

Sara Peterson lived her whole life as a good girl until she uprooted her life and moved to Dallas with her friends. Her life was turned upside down when her friends talked her into walking into Fetish, a BDSM club. Sara discovers more than she expected: a new life that calls to her and a Dom that drives her crazy.

Terrance Williams has always been married to his career until one night, he was struck dumb by a blonde-haired smart mouth. He would give almost anything to tie her up with his rope. No matter what he does, she drifts farther away. Will she surrender to his will? Or will he be the one tied up in knots?

Releasing March 31st. 2024

Brenna Hayes is a very busy woman. She develops app software for all electronics, trains Doms and Submissives, and helps her dear friends LaMarkus and Faye in the Fetish club when needed. Now, she has just opened a school of kink with her friends. Will she be able to maintain a healthy and stable life? Or will her life start spinning out of control?

Adrian Hayes is a simple man...all he wants is a simple life with the woman he fell in love with over twenty years ago. It was love at first sight to Adrian when he stumbled across Brenna when she was visiting Ireland. When he thought things would settle for them, something else that tried to put a wedge between them popped up. Will Adrian be content with what he has?

Or will he go home to Ireland after twenty years of being a loving husband and devoted submissive to Brenna?

Releasing May 31st 2024

S. E. Olson

URBAN ROMANCE AUTHOR.

Check out the new Urban Romance Author. Her debut Novel will be released in 2024.

After losing the love of his life and the mother of his children, Darius Wilks deems himself emotionally unavailable. Darius has to make the decision to leave the drug game and the big city and change his life for his daughters. After walking into the hospital room of one of his clients, he sees a cardiothoracic attending surgeon, Samantha Wilson, and is mesmerized.

Can she change his Emotionally Unavailable status?

Leigh Titler

Amazon Best Selling Dark Fantasy/ Paranormal Romance Author

Aadya's Curse...

This is the story of three sisters...and about love and betrayal. Travel with these sisters as they face obstacles and secrets of their past. On their journey, Temperance Jade and Zeke feel sparks. Will Zeke be put off by Temperance's smart mouth? Or will Temperance accept Zeke's Dominance?

Aadya's Curse Continues...

Returning to Aadya follows the story as Temperance, Acelyn, and the others race to Aadya to save Zanderley from the evil Morgana. Along the way, while Anton works to win her heart, Acelyn battles her own issues of trust.

Aadya's Curse concludes...

Aadya's Battle finishes the story of three sisters reunited and fighting for what matters most. Amid weddings and coronations, will Zanderley Coda come together so all three sisters face the future with their mates by their side?

Kayah was orphaned at a young age when her parents were killed by the Hunters, a rival bike club. The only reason the Alpha of the Dire Wolves took in a Timberwolf pup was out of respect for her father. Fight with Kayah while she fights for her respect not only in the pack but for her spot in the Biker Club as well. When the Hunters attack, will Kayah help save the family that raised her? As her twenty-first birthday slowly creeps closer, will Kayah find her mate, or will she be shunned for life because she is the only Timberwolf of a Dire Wolf pack?

Christmas has always been hard for Kayah, with losing her parents on Christmas Eve. Can her new family help her come to love Christmas and put her past to rest? All for the sake of her unborn child.

Releasing September 2024

Cerilla finds herself in a new world and a slave to another. After years of doing her master's bidding, she escapes to a new world with the wolves. She quickly finds herself alone after being told she cannot live amongst the wolves. She sets her sights on her new obsession that she can't wait to sink her teeth into.

Luca Kennedy is clueless about the evil that is lurking in the dark. Will he fall pray to the bloodthirsty demon that lives at night, or will he meet his end with the hunter hunting him?

Lana Morgan comes from a long line of vampire hunters. She is known for not fooling around and quick kills. When she is given the mission to put Luca down, she runs into problems that make her hesitant. Will she do her job and put him down, or will she follow her heart and surrender to his will?

Printed in Great Britain
by Amazon

42394515R00116